EGON THE BOLD

BLAZE WARD

KNOTTED ROAD PRESS

Egon the Bold
Blaze Ward
Copyright © 2021 Blaze Ward
All rights reserved
Published by Knotted Road Press
www.KnottedRoadPress.com

ISBN: 978-1-64470-218-5

Cover art:

ID 117773721 © Yevgenii Movliev | Dreamstime.com

Reviews
It's true. Reviews help. Even a short one, such as, "Loved it!" So please consider reviewing this book (and all of the ones you've read) on your favorite retailer site.

Never miss a release!
If you'd like to be notified of new releases, sign up for my newsletter.

http://www.blazeward.com/newsletter/

Buy More!
Did you know that you can buy directly from my website?

https://www.blazeward.com/shop/

ALSO BY BLAZE WARD

The Lazarus Alliance

Escape

Return

Rebellion

Revolution

Liberation

Retribution

The Jessica Keller Chronicles

Auberon

Queen of the Pirates

Last of the Immortals

Goddess of War

Flight of the Blackbird

The Red Admiral

St. Legier

Winterhome

Petron

CS-405

Queen Anne's Revenge

Packmule

Persephone

Additional Alexandria Station Stories

Siren

Two Bottles of Wine with a War God

The Story Road

The Science Officer Series Season One

The Science Officer

The Mind Field

The Gilded Cage

The Pleasure Dome

The Doomsday Vault

The Last Flagship

The Hammerfield Gambit

The Hammerfield Payoff

The Bryce Connection

The Science Officer Series Season Two

Alien Seas

Shadow of the Dominion

Longshot Hypothesis

Hard Bargain

Outermost

Dominion-427

Phoenix

Princess Rualoh

For the original Cletus: Thanks for letting me borrow him.

CONTENTS

ONE

UNLIKELY FRIENDS

EGON CONSIDERED his morning oatmeal and tepid beer with something approaching disdain, but if he's wanted to get that first batch of the good stuff this morning, this orc would have had to get his lazy, green ass out of bed before the dawn like he usually did. Today just hadn't been that day.

Life didn't always require an hour of prayer to start his day, but it was a habit that had been ground into his hard head for nearly a decade at this point, since he had first taken up his vows. The Goddess would generally not stint on blessing him with her power if he missed a morning, but it better not become a habit, mister.

He just hadn't felt the need to get up today. Too tired. Too something.

So the morning risers had gotten the good oatmeal. He was kind of scraping the bottom of the big pot at this point. Sure, he had a few extra silver in his pouch, had he really wanted to eat fresh eggs and maybe a ham steak, but again, sleeping in had been a choice he'd made when that first stupid rooster had decided everyone else had slept long enough.

For the briefest moment, he considered casting a quick, little enchantment on his bowl to give it a better taste. Some spices. Maybe a dash of fruit juice added to cut the wood pulp on his tongue. Something.

But that was the way towards laziness, and Egon the Bold was anything but lazy. The Goddess had called him at a young age. At a time when the other Orcs had started training hard with the blade, he had taken up the hammer, studying at the forge with the other priests and learning her fire and smithing magic.

She had been pleased. But the youngest son of the king had never been one to slack. Shouldn't start now, a decade of hard work later, when she had sent him out into the world to right wrongs and spread her *Word* of hard work and fair play.

So he ate glompy oatmeal that had been on the stove too long and drank that thin, weak beer the Humans liked. The kind with hardly any malt and way too many hops, until it was bitter enough that he had considered using it to strip rust off his plate armor. Not much stronger than water, but he was pretty sure it would kill any mold growing anywhere.

Again, not worth spending precious silver on languor and debauchery. Had he wanted to do that, he could have stayed home in the Royal Hall with his brothers and their friends.

"Begging your illustrious pardon, good sir?" a voice broke in on his reverie.

Egon looked around, but he was alone on this side of the ancient, scarred, wooden bar, standing close enough to lean on while he ate.

"Ahem," the voice came again.

Egon looked down at the man accosting him. He'd say it was way too early to be so chipper, but the man was a Puck. Too damned sunny by nature. One of the smallest of the

Humanoid races, barely three feet tall, and that might require lifts in his pretty boots to achieve.

The Pucks weren't necessarily always bright and cheery, gregarious folk always with a smile, a laugh, and perhaps a dirty joke on their lips, but this one looked like the archetype from which all those old stories might have been originally drawn.

Those boots in a polished black, perhaps with extra heels in them. Maroon pants that left the impression of armor, doubly so when Egon took a second look and noted the way the surface appeared to be scales of leather or metal stitched to an inner layer. White, silk shirt that absolutely had to require magic to keep that clean and pretty in the squalor of this world, covered over with a maroon vest that looked more like an armored doublet to make the pants a matched set.

Being a Puck, he even had the requisite green cloak about his neck, clasped in silver that had been chased with bronze in the form of a leaf. The hood was back and the left side cast rakishly over a shoulder, displaying a fine, thin blade that looked like the sort of thing Egon might use to clean his tusks and maybe get between some of his back teeth in a pinch.

Pucks didn't grown facial hair, just like gnomes and some of the more fey-related folk, so they all looked young. Egon had just enough beard these days to pass for an adult. Nineteen going on forty, as his mother had liked to say.

And he could feel a headache coming on, just considering what this bright, friendly fellow might want with a slightly sour Orc in heavy armor, carrying a blessed hammer on his hip.

"Cletus T. Colville, at your service, good sir," he smiled, with a theatrical bow, looking like a Puck with three magic beans in a cloth bag that he needed to sell quickly to an enterprising young lad.

Mother had warned him about con artists and showmen. She might have met this fellow in a previous life, since Pucks like him tended to live so much longer than simple Orcish folk.

Egon considered what was left of his bowl and his beer. Not enough to justify abandoning it, even with a Puck on the prowl. And Mother had beaten better manners into him, back when he had been a prince.

He nodded to the fellow, scooped the second to last bite and chewed rapidly.

Hopefully the Puck would go away. Might require Egon asking the Goddess for a spell to banish curses and malevolent beings first, though. Pucks could be like that.

"I see that you are about your breakfast, but I felt that I might still impose upon you for a moment if you did not have a prior commitment today?" Cletus T. Colville went right into his spiel.

Egon looked around for backup moving in to pick his pocket when he was distracted. They frequently worked in pairs. Egon would outweigh any four of them with his armor, shield, and hammer tossed onto the scale.

"Egon," he replied by way of gruff introduction.

Strangers, ill met in a rough bar, on the edge of a tired city, in a kingdom meandering down into senescence and futility as dark things from the east probed at the civilized lands.

"Indeed," Cletus's smile got even bigger. "Egon the Bold, if I might be so forward. Your name and glories precede you, fine sir."

Egon doubted it. Nobody this far south should have even heard of him. And a Puck in the old country would have stood out. Granted, he'd been gone for over a year now, so perhaps wandering minstrels and other fools had heard about that one thing and gone ahead and turned it into a legendary epic when nobody stopped them.

They did that when you left them alone with their rhymes.

Villagers had been beset and sent a messenger for help. Egon had just happened to arrive before the right Court on the right day to present himself to a minor king and been suddenly tasked with cleaning out a nest of skeletons someone had awakened or released from some forgotten tomb.

The Blessing of the Goddess was a powerful thing, in the hands of her favored. And she did like him well enough to answer his prayers with power. So he'd gone ahead and been a hero.

Egon shrugged and grunted. The last bite could probably wait, if this silly, tiny fellow—whose shoulders were about even with Egon's knees—was about to wind himself up into some tale that had grown beyond itself in the making up.

He grabbed his beer and drank most of what was left to try to thin the wood pulp on his tongue.

"And what might I do for you today, Master Colville?" Egon finally asked, turning to put his back against the bar. It would trap his shield, but that in turn would protect him if some other Puck decided to jump up on the wooden barricade.

This Puck smiled like a djinn released from his bottle.

"You, sir, are an *adventurer*," Cletus announced in a voice Egon would have preferred be quieter.

Around here, that term had mercenary overtones that didn't always sit well. Some folks would look askance on him as a paid warrior, while others might be of the opinion that they could hire him to do things for them.

Requests Egon might find morally objectionable.

Egon had put his spoon down with his bowl, so he

reached out and touched the head of his blessed hammer, with the Goddess's sigil worked into the sides of the head in bronze.

"I am a priest, good fellow," he countered in a low, almost menacing voice, not mentioning the well-worn gear or the expensive plate armor he wore.

Had he a sword on his hip or an ax across his back, he might well be mistaken for one of his poorer cousins, headed south into the world to make his fortune and fame.

"Indeed," Cletus grinned even wider. "Of course. One who specializes in destroying fell creatures emerging from the night to rend and shatter."

Egon wondered if he would pull something, rolling his eyes too hard at the glib man and his fancy tones.

"And?" he cut to the chase.

"And I was wondering how you felt about a business proposition, my fine man," Cletus pivoted just as rapidly to the brass tacks portion of a morning that Egon really wanted to have slept in even longer and avoided.

Egon scowled at the fellow. Eyes, mouth, even tusks.

Pucks were notoriously immune to that sort of thing, unlike so many other Humanoids.

Still, something got through to the little man. Perhaps Pucks could hear quieter growls than most as well.

He bowed adroitly.

"Perhaps after you have finished your breakfast and had a moment to digest," he suggested, taking a half step backwards in the process. "I shall retire to yon corner table and await your curiosity with great enthusiasm."

At least he did walk away, grinning and jaunty, but away.

Egon was just glad he didn't have a hangover this morning. That on top of a Puck with a magic cow to sell you might be asking too much.

He turned back to his breakfast with a grumbly sigh.

Adventurers were just fancy mercenaries. He was at least called by the Goddess, even if he did occasionally accept coin for his work, at least when he didn't end up finding a stash of coins at the bottom of a catacomb after some asshole necromancer had gotten above himself and started just unleashing skeletons on the countryside.

As a result of his efforts, there was one less wizard in the world this month, seducing himself for whatever night gods wanted to offer him power.

Egon finished his oatmeal and scraped the bowl clean with the wooden spoon. Yuck, but life never promised you fritatas and dancing girls. At least not after you left your palace home.

The beer went with it. Egon belched and wondered if he would have been better off just filling his waterskin from the well and invoking a purification on it to kill off anything swimming in it.

If he stayed in his place much longer, he was going to break down and start spending his hoard of coins on better victuals. Which would run them down again, necessitating that he listen to business propositions from happy Pucks awake too early.

And maybe head out into the east to smash undead creatures and their masters. The kind that weren't willing to let the old wars be.

That land had been an Empire once, over the river and past whatever haunted forests had sprung up. A proud, shining beacon that had sought to unite all peoples into a greater glory, at least until an idiot, third son decided to start killing people around him, the ones who had a better claim to the throne. And then hiring people to follow him into outright rebellion when that failed.

Civil wars were nasty, ugly things. This one had drawn in several orders of wizards, a couple of dragons, and supposedly most of the gods before it ended. As had nearly all of the people across the river.

At least *this* idiot third son knew better. Egon the Bold was a priest, not a rebel. Maybe a hero, but right now he needed a piss.

He nodded in a bemused way to the Puck, belched in the general direction of the publican with a smile, and headed for the rear door to the jakes.

HUMAN PISS WAS A NASTY SMELL. Egon wondered what they might need to change in their diet to reduce the rankness as he emerged feeling at least somewhat refreshed and looked around the small, packed-dirt quad behind the inn.

Someone was up to no good. Six someones, from the looks of it.

They didn't look like simple thieves. All of them wore armor of various qualities, ranging from leather with metal studs up to one industrious fool of a Human wearing a scale tunic originally made for an Orc Egon's size. It hung on him like a blanket, even with a belt around the man's waist.

And all of them had weapons in hand. Swords, axes, and even a mace. Three Humans, two Elves, and a Dwarf with a helmet that had goat horns coming out of it. Egon hoped they were attached to the helmet and not the Dwarf.

The Dwarf looked like the leader of this little tribe of miscreants. He had as much hair on his body as all the rest of them combined, and a two-handed ax that had seen better days.

"Yer kind're no welcome here," the Dwarf snarled in what Egon supposed was meant to sound tough.

Would have helped it he had tusks under all that beard.

8

Egon felt like he was being threatened by an angry badger with a slight case of mange. One of the southern ones that looked like it was about to invite you to tea, rather than the kind up north where he came from, where they looked like they were about to follow you down a dark alley and mug you for three coppers and your boots.

Still, six on one. Not even remotely sporting odds. And in the backyard of the inn calling down the flaming ire of the goddess would probably piss off the publican. Doubly so if he managed to set the entire block on fire.

Egon sighed. He smiled.

Rather than argue with the fellow, he reached back and pulled his shield forward onto his left arm and cast a small blessing. Nothing much, just a slight adjustment in how the world flowed.

If you never attack me, you won't even notice how your luck has changed.

He didn't draw the hammer. That might provoke them, when he might still have a chance to slip out of this confrontation without blood being shed.

Egon watched the Dwarf and wondered if he should have asked the Goddess this morning for the ability to call down lightning bolts. The chain mail on the Dwarf would look wonderful, all lit up.

"Ya hear me, boy?" the Dwarf roared a little louder.

This wasn't a Dwarven kingdom. There was one dominated brutally by those folks farther to the west. And they occasionally got pissy with their Orquish neighbors. This kingdom here was more of a crossroads where travelers of all stripes and sizes met, largely dominated by Humans.

Still, the Goddess had led his feet to this place. She must have something interesting planned.

Egon wasn't sure he would enjoy it, but he was her servant.

"I hear your yammering, furball," Egon answered, inching towards unleashing the Goddess's holy fire on these uncouth shits. "Do you have a point, or are you just common brigands wandered in from the swamp to foul the carpets around here."

My, my, my. Sensitive spot?

Egon wondered if the Dwarf was about to actually start frothing from the growls and gnashing coming through those missing teeth.

The bastard howled some curse and charged, catching his cohorts completely off-guard, as they weren't ready to fight an Orc taller than them and wearing better armor.

At least Egon had an outhouse behind him, so nobody could sneak into his blind spot.

The frothing Dwarf swung with both hands.

Egon didn't bother trying to get his hammer out. He took a half-step and deflected the ax to one side as it descended.

"Curse you," the furball snarled as the ax buried itself in the packed dirt of the yard.

Egon considered punching the fucker in the face, but the punk still had five friends who weren't sure about all this, so maybe it would be possible to get out of this with just a few insults exchanged.

And then the Dwarf's eyes started to glow red. Never a good sign. Doubly so before lunch.

"Ganchette bless me with your power," he howled.

Something *dark* answered, just in the way the shadows seemed to stir and a chill breeze sprang up around them.

The Goddess was not the mortal enemy of Ganchette the Stygian, but they were rarely on the same sides of *any* discussion. And this Dwarf wasn't just a brigand. Bastard was apparently a harridan of some sort. Not a priest, blessed by a greater being like Egon, but someone who had entered a dark pact for raw power, somewhere along the way.

The ax began to glow with that same red power. And his five friends finally woke up and started moving forward.

Egon drew his hammer and set his feet. The day might just end with him asking the Goddess to send rain to put out the shit he wondered if he was going to have to start here.

The ugly, glowing Dwarf had stumbled, getting his axhead out of the dirt, so he was slow and off-balance. Egon considered doing something, but that would end up with him surrounded by the other five.

Screw that.

He stepped to his right and launched a kick at the guy holding the longsword in two hands. Leather armor with studs was nice, but the fool had skipped the codpiece. Steel greaves on an Orcy shin connected with his danglies at high speed.

Looked painful. Sounded that way, too, from the sudden screaming.

Egon pivoted back as the Elf with the mace rushed in. Shield took most of it. Pauldron took the rest.

Egon still hadn't pulled the hammer. He'd probably lose his temper when he did.

He punched the Elf in the gob instead. Elves were almost as tall as Orcs, far skinnier. Almost pretty, even the boys. This one was going to need a healer for his nose, if he didn't want one of his buddies setting it wrong and making him ugly.

Another healer. Egon would make sure it was off-center if he ended up curing the moron after all this was done.

The Dwarf did something else ugly. Egon wasn't sure, but he hadn't spent a lot of time studying the various powers of a harridan to know what they supposedly could do. Partly, it likely came down to whatever an asshole god like Ganchette the Stygian granted to his favored.

The Dwarf started to glow all over, and not just his eyes. This glow was golden. Didn't look like fun.

He overhanded the ax again, telegraphing everything practically in slow motion. Egon considered taking advantage of that and stepping into it, blocking with the shield so he could punch the little shit, but that glow in the fool's eyes suggested that the furry bastard was just waiting for something like that.

Instead of getting close and punching him, Egon stepped back and let the blow go by.

Smart idea, from the explosion of turf and mud when the ax went to the head in the dirt again, blinding everyone. Knocked the Dwarf on his ass, along with the other Elf.

Scale-mail-scarecrow decided to try his luck. Or something.

A glowing red demon suddenly emerged from that hole in the ground and charged at the guy howling.

Egon would have expected a summoning like that to come this way instead, but then he saw that grinning Puck slip out the back door of the inn and slide right up being the flailing Human. Demon must have been an illusion. Damned good one too, from the way the guy freaked out.

Vicious, little smiling Puck came in close behind him and punched the Human in the back of the knee. Followed that up with a dagger pommel right on top of the suddenly-accessible skull as the man lurched backwards.

Sounded like a melon dropped out of a second story window. Scarecrow collapsed, thrashing a little.

The Dwarf was getting his act together again. Still on his butt. Still glowing. Still had that ax in hand. Moving slowly as he tried to get up.

Egon decided he'd finally had enough.

He looked at the last Human standing right now and

invoked a tiny fraction of the power the Goddess had granted him.

"Flee," he commanded the man, letting his black eyes glow bright golden fire.

It was a safe enough enchantment to drop on someone you didn't know. Weak-willed fool blinked, screamed, and started running, tripping blindly over a sudden foot a particular Puck had stuck out.

Bad trip. Face-plant into the side of the building kind of trip.

Egon wondered if the man had managed to break his fool neck. Might have to actually heal him too if that was the case.

Egon the Bold. Not Egon the Asshole.

Dwarf was up again.

Man, that furball was pissed.

Egon didn't even recognize the chanting, but it wasn't Dwarven. Fire-forge clerics learn many tongues reading the ancient tomes, from the ideograms of the dragons to the cursive of the fire gnomes.

This sounded like evil. Or the calling down of evil.

Egon looked at the rest of the band. They were down. Or hurling up breakfast in the case of the guy who was probably going to go buy himself an armored codpiece in the afternoon.

Egon pulled the hammer finally.

Felt it glow with the Goddess's blessing. Little flames appeared around the head.

He wondered if that beard would burn.

Harridan cast something else now. Actually stopped ranting and swinging long enough to hold out a hand, palm pointed at Egon with some bad shit coming.

"No, I don't think so," Cletus spoke up, gesturing at the Dwarf.

Egon felt the surge of magical power from the friendly Puck, but it wasn't aimed at him, so he wasn't sure what the guy had done.

The Dwarf was sure. He went to his knees, screaming and clutching his head.

At least he dropped the ax.

Egon ignored the ax and whomped the Dwarf on the top of the skull, right between the horns. The frothing punk had a helmet. Hopefully those horns were decorative and not part of the Dwarf.

Down came Egon's mighty hammer, right on the man's crown. The hardest part of the head. Hopefully soft enough to not go squish. Seemed sufficient, as the screaming stopped and the Dwarf fell over.

Egon looked at the weapon, but all the enchantments had faded, so it wasn't an unholy weapon. Just a thing held by an unholy punk.

He considered hurling it end over end like a dagger, just to see how far it would fly, but there were fences on all sides. Clearing one of them with a throw put someone else at risk downrange.

"Allow me?" Cletus beamed.

A magical, glowing hand came into existence and the ax suddenly lofted into the air. Egon watched it gently fly up to the pitched roof of the inn and come to rest next to a drain gargoyle.

Egon looked around. Most of the punks seemed just out of it for now, so he dropped a quick cure on the one who might have broken his neck. Wasn't time for proper medicine, if a couple of his friends might still be feeling feisty in a few moments.

He rolled the Human over to make sure his eyes still focused.

"Don't follow me, or next time you'll end up in hell," he told the man in a bright voice. "Savvy?"

The man nodded energetically so Egon dropped him and rose to his full seven feet of height.

"That goes for all of you," he said in a loud enough voice that a bard three blocks down might turn it into another legend by Thursday. "Next time I see any of your faces, I'm going to get ugly and assume it was self-defense. And it's not cannibalism afterwards, since none of you are Orcs."

Egon turned to go and found Cletus falling into stride next to him, those stubby legs churning madly to keep up.

"Thank you," Egon nodded as they got inside the inn.

"Indeed it was my pleasure, good sir," Cletus replied. "That gentleman back there with the ax was part of the reason I wanted to engage with you this morning. He's a bit of a hard-headed fellow, and worships a chap I find rather objectionable. Plus, I have this map that I acquired, purportedly leading to some lost and hidden treasure that said gentleman was intent upon reclaiming. One presumes that a person of such moral standing as he would be up to all manner of mischief, were he to lay hands upon it again."

"I see," Egon replied. "And your thought with engaging my services?"

"If Vorlothe the Dwarf wants whatever the map leads one to, then it should probably be destroyed," Cletus turned serious for the first time. Even his voice dropped down. "I think a forge priest would be the perfect companion on such a journey. Some things are too evil to be allowed to exist."

Egon could agree with that. Unmaking things was almost as important to the Goddess as making them. Some of the other gods had gotten a little out of hand with the powers they had granted mortals over the centuries.

"I think it would be best if we stayed elsewhere," Cletus

said as they crossed the main room. "If you are amenable, we shall send someone for our things later."

Egon watched him toss a gold coin to the publican as they passed.

"Sorry about the mess out back," he said cheerfully. "I'll explain later."

And then they were out the front door and onto a cobblestone lane.

Cletus stopped and looked up at him.

"Can I buy you a better meal with Orcish beer while we chat about good and evil, my friend?" the Puck asked.

"Yes," Egon decided. "That would be good."

The Goddess had sent his steps this way. Apparently she had need of his hammer and his faith.

As did the rest of them.

TWO

BUILDING THE FAITH

EGON THE BOLD considered the gloriously bright and witty Puck seated on one point of a triangle, around a round table in a better dive than the one he'd been staying at previously. Cletus T. Colville, with the T. so far short for three different things when Egon had asked at various times. But the smiling, little man was like that. Just naturally exuberant enough that even a normally-dour Orc had to smile.

On the third point of the triangle was a Human woman. Ilvash Marrove. Like him, just finishing up a lunch of roast beef served on slices of good bread, with stewed veggies on the side. Some of them he even recognized. A mug of good stout sat half-empty at his right hand. All of it far better than the thin oatmeal and watery beer that had been breakfast.

The woman was so petite that Egon had originally wondered if she was a skinny Dwarf or a tall Puck, but apparently Humans could be a petite four foot ten and that was normal. At seven feet even, Egon felt like a giant standing next to the other two.

She had red hair, almost carrot colored and cut no longer

than his even though she didn't put it under a helmet, plus freckles, which was generally a Human thing. Smart as a whip cracking, too.

At home in the Northern Court where Egon was a third son of a king, she'd have been a scholar of some note, even though she didn't look any older than him. Journeyman Enchanter was the term she'd used, but Egon wasn't familiar with these southerners and their exotic ways.

The Goddess had set his feet southward, until his trail crossed Mr. Colville's this morning and the two of them had gone on to have a nasty encounter with a Dwarf who worshiped Ganchette the Stygian. Several of the Dwarf's friends had not saved him getting his ass kicked, though.

Egon studied the Puck now, not ignoring the woman, but focusing his question on the man. She hadn't been there, having slept in, but apparently was another fellow traveler on the quest Cletus had set himself to.

"You promised a discussion on good and evil earlier," Egon prompted.

"So I did, so I did," Cletus nodded, taking a long drink of his beer. "You have now met my old foe, Vorlothe the Dwarf. I think in the north the term you use to describe such a person is a Harridan, yes?"

"Correct," Egon agreed. "Not filled with the blessing of the deity each morning, but granted some aspects of power, dedicated to a cause."

"Indeed you are correct, sir," Cletus replied. "Southerners generally use the term Oathsworn. Unfortunately, many of them choose to bargain with darker powers, rather than serve true gods. Demons and the like. Ganchette the Stygian was mortal once, but managed to accumulate enough power to possibly live forever."

"Demigod?" Egon asked.

"He has not *Ascended* to true godhead," Ilvash finally

spoke up. "Nor gone the path of lichdom to become the undying either. He cannot sustain many such supporters as the Dwarf, but enough to sow chaos wherever he goes."

"I see," Egon muttered. "And the map you mentioned? The one leading to some treasure needing to be *unmade*?"

"Power is power," Cletus replied, finally turning serious for the first time in more than an hour. "The various gods fought a few wars in previous centuries, and things got a little out of hand. They cannot harm each other directly, as a rule. Such is the nature of godhead itself. But they can alter the balance of power among their kind by making their own cult stronger or the others weaker."

"Weaker?" Egon asked.

"If someone killed all the followers of Brese, your Forge Goddess, she would no longer have nearly as much influence in the world," Cletus said. "Much of her power is drawn from the faith of her servants, offered up in prayers that she might use it to make the world a better place."

"That would require many, many deaths," Egon pointed out.

"So it would," Cletus agreed. "Now, consider if one of the other beings granted one of his followers a powerful weapon, a sword that didn't just kill its foes, but perhaps absorbed their souls and granted that power to a mortal. Then other gods decided to get into the act, unwilling to be outshone."

"You're talking about the Slayer Wars," Egon realized. "But those ended six hundred years ago."

"They did," Cletus nodded. "The Gillanish Empire rose when the last of the dark cults was finally destroyed. But, as with all things, it eventually succumbed to evil in turn, and was destroyed in a civil war that nobody ended up winning, except places in the west like this, not important enough to sack then, and barely hanging on as a trade route between the northern kingdoms where you were born, and the southern lands beyond this."

"And your map?" Egon pressed.

Cletus smiled slyly now. Egon smelled a pig in a poke and wondered if he was already done with this conversation.

"Technically, not my map, except as how possession at present might rule in my favor, were the situation to come before certain magistrates tasked with upholding such things," the Puck replied, circuitously as always. "Before me, it might have been in the possession of a certain Dwarf, of whom you most recently made an unfortunate acquaintance."

"What he's saying is that he stole it from Vorlothe," Ilvash inserted, giving the Puck a rather dirty look in the process. "Vorlothe might not have known until now who had it, but he's recruiting a small company to go into the *darkwilds* and will be coming after Cletus in force soon."

"Indubitably," Cletus smiled and nodded. "Thus it behooves me to locate associates, heroes of a certain ethical posture, that we might resist such an incursion, perhaps going so far as to harry our foes along the way and swooping in to prevent them from achieving their dread goal."

Egon's head was going to start hurting if he had to listen to this sorts of nattering constantly, but he suspected that it was a nervous tic on the Puck's part. The more excited and emotional he got, the more syllables were required to actually communicate a simple thing.

"You mentioned specifically needing a forge cleric," Egon decided to cut to the chase. "Why?"

"A previous group, possibly allied with Ganchette, possibly some other fell creature, penetrated a certain depth into the *darkwilds*, master cleric," Cletus replied. "Their casualties were stunningly bad, and only two survivors managed to limp home, having charted as far as they made it, plus a bit more with the aid of certain divination magics. They intended to find more help, but found a notorious Dwarf instead, and are no more."

"Divinations?" Egon asked, turning to Ilvash now.

He was a cleric, a somewhat lowly warrior priest sworn into Brese's service. She might give him a sign in a dream, or direct him with a nudge, but he had not earned her trust to the point that she would part the veils to show him visions of the future.

The woman grimaced and nodded.

"Whoever did it was more powerful than I, sir," she admitted, possibly rather painfully. "But few would take up a quest this dangerous. Most of my kind are content to build small towers and sell enchanted trinkets to travelers, while paying explorers in gold for such things as they might recover from such undertakings."

"And your reason?" Egon pressed, feeling a particularly Orcy glower coming over his face.

"If I survive, I shave a decade off of how long it might normally take me to do the same," she said with a hard edge to her voice. "Most enchanters tend to be male, and chauvinist pigs who do not believe that a woman has the drive to succeed."

"More the fools them," Egon replied, thinking back to his sainted mother, who kept his father's Court on a short leash and a balanced budget.

But the southerners did not see the Orc kingdoms of the north as sophisticated places. They only saw the mercenaries that came south for adventure, glory, and money.

Egon was willing to admit to two of those, if pressed.

He turned back to Cletus now.

"So what did the map show?" he asked bluntly. "What was the treasure that would draw in so many, like flies on a rotting corpse?"

Cletus actually grimaced now. He paused to empty his wee mug of stout and wipe his mouth before leaning forward.

"I will mention a name now, but it should not be spoken frequently," he said. "You never know what ears might be listening. It will be safe now. I have left a few illusions about to confuse those who might seek me."

"Go on," Egon said.

"*Ediade*," he murmured. "Once born into battle by a champion named…"

"Arinwa Hollenc," Egon interrupted quietly, scowling so broadly he wondered if his tusks might touch his eyebrows.

"You are familiar with the history, then?" Cletus asked, a bit surprised from the way his eyes got big.

"I am," Egon said. He paused to shoot a look at the Human to include her in the conversation. "I'm in."

"We have not even discussed pay or shares, Egon," Cletus tried to deflect him.

"We have not," Egon agreed. "I'm sure things will be equitable enough, at the end of the day."

"Then you ready to engage?"

"This is evil that must be destroyed," Egon stated. "Finally, and forever."

EGON HAD NOT DEVELOPED A PARTICULARLY high opinion of the city of Teregossa while he'd been here. Nor the kingdom it was the capital of. But he supposed that endlessly facing the magically-dangerous lands of the *darkwilds* would leave anybody a bit sour.

Merchants took a look at him and saw just another big fool adventurer going off to die, since so few of them returned wealthy and successful. He didn't bother reminding them that anybody striking it rich out there wouldn't advertise it here. Hell, he'd tell everyone he'd barely got out with his life as he announced his retirement, just before he headed somewhere else with a backpack so full of gold coin and treasure that he waddled when he walked.

Egon didn't really need much in the way of supplies. Everything he'd brought south with him was largely intact, and he'd taken a few jobs along the way that provided him with enough spare coin that he could avoid dipping into the stuff hidden in his boots and inside his breastplate.

What fools walked around a city like this announcing he had money? Southerners were weird that way.

But he'd volunteered to escort Ilvash into the market district to pick up a few supplies while Cletus inquired about town for a fourth person he thought would round things out nicely.

Egon wore his heavy armor, even including the helmet, with his shield slung across his back and the hammer hanging on his belt. He had a nice outfit for Court or such, rolled up in oilcloth if he needed it, but nobody down here needed to know that he was anything but another bum passing through. And after yesterday, there was no such thing as too paranoid around here.

Ilvash, at least, didn't look like an enchanter. Someone had done a pretty good job of dressing the tiny, Human woman in leathers that looked like real armor, down to the rivets in various places. Up close, he could tell that that lacked the heft or toughness to be of any great benefit if she was attacked, but it didn't scream Enchanter when you looked at her.

Similarly, the light sword she wore on her hip was mostly for show, as she'd admitted she could barely swing it. At least she claimed to reasonably competent with the small crossbow she had left at the inn, so that might help. Overall, she looked like the sorts of wilderness scout someone like Cletus might hire for this sort of expedition. If you weren't looking too closely.

Keeping fools at a respectable distance was his job, anyway.

"What are we looking for, again?" he asked, mostly because the afternoon was wearing on and the market crowd was starting to thin out now.

Plus, she couldn't generally see over the shoulders of the largely-Human crowd around them, while Egon could see over heads. There had only been three people his height that he's seen today. Another Orc, what looked like a skinny ogre woman, and an honest to goodness troll, although Egon didn't think they ever traveled this far south.

But the man had been a merchant of some sort, mostly selling hides of exotic creatures, along with this and that. Nothing Egon had needed, but he'd paused, just to check.

"Herbs and a few minerals," she muttered back. "Ingredients for potions and poultices for the most part."

"Bear left a few points," he offered. "There is a table in the corner that looks promising. Next to the candlemaker."

"Oh, I need some tallow as well." She snapped her finger. "Thank you for the reminder."

Egon walked heavy. Loud, in a jingly, thumping kind of way that let people know he was coming. It tended to open a corridor in front of Ilvash, which made their work faster.

He hadn't forgotten yesterday morning, and the altercation near the north gate. Nor the Dwarf and his friends. Cletus had mentioned that he thought they would be safe closer to the eastern marketplace, but Egon kept his eyes sweeping back and forth.

It was one thing to hide from pickpockets and brigands, but a Harridan, Oathsworn in the south, was a different thing, as Egon had no idea what magics the man might invoke. Or what his patron might offer.

A woman emerged from the stillness of the crowd around him. Nearby, Ilvash came to rest near a table and began a conversation with the Elf behind it so complicated that it might have been another language.

Egon studied the newcomer. Merchant's wife, from the way she was dressed, in clothing a little finer and cleaner than most. Human, a head taller than Ilvash, with brown hair in a braid and skin much darker than the enchanter as well. Almost old oak in color.

She studied him for a long moment.

"Brese?" she asked, a little surprise lurking in her eyes as she studied the logo worked on his chest piece. The hammer and anvil icon of the goddess.

Egon nodded.

"Are times so bad, then, that she calls the faithful down from the north again?" the woman asked tensely, as if Egon would understand what she was talking about.

Egon looked closer and noted a necklace in silver around her neck, with a hammer icon hanging from it.

A believer.

"Only this one, mother fair," he replied to the woman in a serious tone, wondering what she saw.

"Then she must believe you sufficient," she replied with a relieved smile.

Egon hefted his hammer and offered her a blessing rather than say anything else. She nodded and vanished into the crowd as though the tide had just turned, leaving him standing there a little confused when Ilvash stepped close and looked up.

"Is everything all right?" she asked.

Egon wasn't sure. He felt like something portentous had just happened, but that he'd been looking the wrong way, for lack of a better way to describe it. Almost as if the old parables about the Goddess herself coming down into the world in disguise, just to interact with someone.

But she wouldn't do that for him? Would she?

Was this the start of something more than just another job to make the world a little better than it had been yesterday?

Egon didn't know. He shook his head and studied Ilvash for a moment.

"I think so, but I could really use a beer right now," he said instead. "You got what you need?"

"Yup, and he even had tallow," she said as she started walking again.

Then he heard something.

Maybe it was because he was still holding his hammer and had been so focused on the other woman. Egon wasn't sure, even later.

But there was a sound over the background hum of the ground and the day. He didn't even know what it was. Automatically, he reached up and unhooked the loop holding his shield onto his back and slid it down his left arm in a single motion as he stepped forward and wrapped his shield arm around Ilvash.

Time seemed to nearly stop as he moved.

An arrow lofted across the space, coming right at her. He had heard the string thrum on release. That had been the sound. His ears had understood even before his brain did.

Egon slid his hammer hand around her as well. He picked the tiny Human up before she could react, turning even more to one side.

The arrow slammed into his shield and bounced downward, splintering as it did.

A howl of rage arose from nearby. It matched the squawk of surprise coming from Ilvash.

Egon scanned all directions quickly and started jogging towards one of the outer walls of the keep, located nearby in between tables and permanent shops.

"What are you doing?" Ilvash demanded angrily.

"Saving your life," Egon said. He set her down and turned around to see a mob of men coming at him. "Stay behind me and make sure nobody jumps down from the wall on my back."

Had that been the Goddess? Had Brese herself foreseen the need for this? Warned him obliquely that he would need his hammer shortly?

Egon didn't recognize any of the men rushing at him from the group he'd beaten up yesterday with Cletus's help, but that didn't mean anything. They were common brigands, ill met and swinging steel. A dozen for a gold piece when times were tough like this.

He turned his head to the one with the bow, standing on a balcony where several shops shared a building.

Elf. Because of course they had hired one of the forest folk, renowned with the bow. The Elf was just stringing a second arrow. He would take another shot at Ilvash as soon as Egon was cornered by the mob.

Egon said a quick prayer to the Goddess and invoked her power in the manifestation of the protection goddess. Mistress of the Forge and the fires that create.

Egon the Bold reached out with a spell and ignited the Elf's bow. The archer dropped it, but not fast enough to escape his hands and the side of his face being scorched. It would probably leave a scar, but the man could not attack again without coming down here in person.

The first brigand swung a mace. Egon hadn't been ignoring them as they closed, but all he needed to do right now was to keep them from getting by him to where they could hurt Ilvash. Another swung a sword. Several more could not approach past the chokepoint that was a seven foot tall, two hundred and fifty pound Orc, wearing another hundred pounds of metal in armor and weapons.

A dam that would hold against any flood of evil.

Sparks flew from his shield, nearly blinding him, but Egon just ducked his head and let the brow of his helmet protect his eyes.

Calmly discussing their differences like rational adults sounded like a choice these men had already skipped over at breakfast, but Egon wasn't immediately intent of killing all of them. That wasn't what a forge cleric did.

Instead, he feinted with his shield and hooked a leg of the man on the right, a Human with his sword clasped in both hands. Egon pulled and the man tumbled, staggering into the one behind him and knocking both down.

The Elf with the mace cursed and swung again. Badly. He barely knew how to grip such a weapon. Egon wondered if his normal weapon of choice was a sap. The other men had that feel to them.

Before Egon could do anything, he felt a hand on the small of his back, and a hand came into his peripheral vision. A rainbow of light exploded in the Elf's face and suddenly he seemed confused. Blinded perhaps, because he started randomly swinging his mace and managed to brain the Human behind him.

Four down, at least for the moment. And it inspired him to do something.

"Lady Brese, blind their eyes," Egon called, holding his hammer up and sending a pulse of magic like a blue wave across the mob in front of him.

Several took on a faint glow and nervously studied hands and weapons, unsure what the big, scary Orc had just done.

Egon smiled and dropped to a knee long enough to punch the Human in the stomach with a mailed gauntlet.

With his left hand, he cracked his shield against the face of the Dwarf behind his target, down on his hands and knees and scrabbling for a cutlass.

Not Vorlothe, which was a shame, but both went down like brained cattle.

Egon rose and studied the three still on their feet. One might still be blind, from the way he swung his mace at anything and everything nearby. Three unconscious at Egon's feet. The archer had vanished from his perch, but Egon wasn't sure where he'd gone.

The crowd was only now realizing that something had gone wrong with their afternoon. Screams and cries of fear started to rise. People began to move away from where he stood, like a tide receding.

Three on one, then. No, make that three on two, as Ilvash had apparently prepared her enchantments for the day.

A howl behind him caused Egon to shuffle to his left a little, just so he could peek behind him.

Ilvash was screaming, possibly in a language he didn't know.

She raised both her hands over her head now as everyone seemed to freeze.

"You will fear me!" she yelled.

And transformed into a…what?

Taller than Egon by a few inches. Broader, too, with long arms covered with blue fur and ending in claws like a bear, maybe. The head could be mistaken for the hybrid offspring of a bear and a demon.

Egon looked close, and realized it was an illusion. He could still see the woman in the middle of it, but the cry of rage that came out of the demon bear's voice echoed off the far walls.

He didn't figure he'd ever get another opening like this, so Egon turned and lunged at the closest bandit, whomping him in the face with his fist, rather than killing the fool with his hammer.

Not today. Not *yet* today, anyway.

Man went down, possibly with a broken jaw.

Egon wasn't feeling charitable enough to fix it for the fool, if that was the case.

The other two broke. The closer one pissed himself in fear and surprise, the sudden spike of ammonia flooding the area. But both turned and went running, not even bothering to keep their weapons.

Egon looked down at the four bandits unconscious at his feet. None of them were dead right now, but if Vorlothe was going to keep this up, Egon could see ratcheting things up to killing, next time this happened.

He was a stranger here. A Northerner just come south for work as a mercenary, as far as these people were concerned. He could always admit to being a prince, if he really got into a pinch, but that was a last resort.

Giggles behind him caused Egon to look.

Ilvash was back to her cute, pixie self, chortling merrily.

"I've always wanted to do that," she said.

"Highly effective," Egon acknowledged. "At least as long as you're facing foes smart enough to fall for it."

"Smart enough?"

"A real bear might see a worthy opponent and ignore me," he smiled down at her. "Or a potential mate."

"Oh, right, gotcha," she nodded, sobering. "What do we do with them?"

Egon was tracking sounds approaching. Many men, in armor, jogging in a military formation. City Guard with spears when he looked up and came to rest.

They opened professionally into a line formation and spears came up, pointed at him and Ilvash.

"What's going on here?" a grizzled veteran on the right asked in a hostile voice.

Egon took a deep breath to start explaining, but was interrupted.

He recognized the woman. The merchant's wife from earlier. The one who might secretly be something else, although he wouldn't even whisper that in the darkness.

"These bandits attacked the young woman," she said authoritatively, stepping in between the line of troopers and Egon. "This hero saved her, and even captured most of them, although you let a few get away."

That last part, she had turned her back on Egon and was facing the veteran. Must have been on hell of an interesting look, because the man actually blushed.

"This true?" he looked at Egon and Ilvash now, much chastened.

"It is," Ilvash agreed. "Someone even fired an arrow at me, and it might have killed me but for this man."

A hand rested on his arm and now it was Egon's turn to blush.

He'd been many things in his nineteen years. Idiot third son was the most common term many folk up north had used.

He'd never been a *Hero* before.

"Bandits?" the veteran asked.

"Most likely," Egon spoke now. "A different group attacked me yesterday at the pub where I had been staying. I beat all of them up, as well."

"That was you?" the veteran asked.

Egon shrugged.

"Not looking for trouble," he replied. "Just got hired for some work in the *darkwilds* and was picking up a few things before we left. I'll be gone tomorrow."

At his feet, like the tide coming back in, some of the fools were starting to stir.

"None of them are dead?" the veteran asked.

Egon shrugged again and hung his hammer from his belt.

"I was merely defending myself and the woman," he announced. "No call for lethality today, but if this keeps up, tomorrow might be different."

"Round them all up," the veteran snarled at his troops.

Egon stepped back as the four bandits suddenly got dragged away.

The merchant's wife actually winked at him, but before Egon could react, she stepped back into the crowd and vanished.

Egon cast a quick divination, but nothing the bandits held was magical, not that he was surprised. Except that a hint of light caught his eye.

He turned that direction and saw a longbow, the string snapped and the wood still smoking. He invoked the Goddess's forge for a gallon of pure water that quenched the flames as he picked up the bow.

Possibly ruined now, although he suspected a competent bowyer could fix it, given time, as the magic someone had imbued in it previously had protected the wood some. Egon could still see the carvings someone had spent an entire winter by the fire perfecting.

Ilvash was close at hand.

"The archer?" she asked.

Egon nodded and pointed at the balcony above.

"He was up there, and dropped this when I set him and it on fire," he murmured, turning and gesturing her to join him. "Gone now, but I suspect he's with Vorlothe as more than just another sellsword, so you will need to be wary of elven archers in your future.

"Who was that woman?" she asked. "The one who spoke up for you."

"Just another of the faithful," Egon replied after a moment.

"A stranger speaking up for a stranger?" Ilvash asked.

"That is how we will defeat evil, Ilvash," he replied. "By building the faithful."

THREE
TALLOWMASTER

MORNING, technically. The sun was pretty close to actually rising in front of them, and the road was a lighter strip of gray than the grass and sparse woods on either side.

Egon had his pack on, with his shield attached outside that. Not immediately accessible in an ambush, but he was wearing chain mail with plates, and had his hammer. And the blessing and magic of the Goddess Brese in a pinch.

"Why did we have to get up so early?" Ilvash groaned, walking in front of him as they headed east on the road to Harhn.

"The best adventures always start early," Cletus replied from the head of their little line with a merry lilt to his voice. But the Puck was always like that, near as Egon could tell.

Certainly, it put more of a smile on his own face, but too many people looked at him and saw a grumpy Orc anyway. Less scowling was probably going to be good for him.

"Also," Cletus continued, "evil tends to stay up too late drinking and carousing, and consequently sleeps in frequently. This gives us a chance to slip away from Teregossa without being under direct observation. While I am certain that at least one of yon guards behind us on the wall will be rewarded with coin for his news, it will take time for such to filter through Teregossa's underworld to the right ears. There being only one real road to Harhn, one presumes that our foes will either have to chase us, thereby catching up on the road, or settle for following us at a more leisurely pace."

"Three days walk to Harhn?" Egon asked.

"If one does not push such things," Cletus agreed ambiguously.

"Is one pushing?" Egon pressed, noting that the Puck was possessed of much shorter legs than even the petite Human woman between them.

"For the morning, fine sir, we are indeed attempting to put miles between us and others," Cletus agreed. "The season is generally wrong for traders following our path, as fall will be upon us any day and winter not long behind. Thus we might meet a few stragglers coming in from the east. The wise man seeks to bed down for a long, cold winter now, content in his knitting."

"But we are not wise men, are we?" Ilvash asked with a sarcastic tone.

Egon like the Human enchanter that Cletus had recruited. Smart woman. Well-read, too, which was good as it would give Egon someone to talk books to. Literacy was rather rare in the south, but this idiot third son of a king could read in four languages. Both of his brothers and most of his cousins had been more interested in beer and swordplay.

"We are indeed fools of the highest order," Cletus laughed in response. "To enter the *darkwilds* in the cold, wet season in pursuit of some nefarious goal, but one might even hope that the evil that festers behind us chooses to spend his winter indoors and warm, rather than damp and miserable."

Egon had never crossed into the lands known as the

darkwilds. In the north, a deep range of sharp mountains separated them from the Orcish kingdoms. Down south, a river emerged from the east where those same mountains tapered off, making a sharp turn at Harhn and heading south.

Too many nasty, monstrous things tended to float down the river for it to be much of a trade corridor, but the fortress town at Harhn did mark the eastern edge of Teregossa. Across the river, according to Cletus's map, the *darkwilds* began.

Ahead of him, Ilvash grumbled at Cletus's wordplay, but the woman was the daughter of two enchanters herself, raised wealthy in a fine tower, surrounded by books and servants. Egon had walked south from his home, doing odd jobs when he needed spare coin and chasing off minor villains. Walking into the *darkwilds* wasn't that much of a difference.

After all, the Goddess had set his feet on this road, so he would pursue whatever task she had put before him. Doubly so as he might have even met her, or at least an avatar yesterday…

Behind them, the first mile of a long road had been completed, and they were largely alone. Around them, farmhouses on either side formed a broken wall, with fields out the back doors and cattle and sheep being turned out to graze, now that the sun would be up shortly.

Egon didn't see lanterns in many windows, but this was not a wealthy kingdom, where vagabond sorcerers might earn a few coin permanently illuminating a stone or icon to glow.

Or perhaps the southerns didn't appreciate lanterns that never needed to be refueled. He supposed that around here they could grow far more crops than the north, so might be able to render various plants down for oil, and not entertain those to studied the arcane arts. They only had to look east across the river to be reminded of what happened when too many wizards gathered power to themselves.

It was not his land, so he would not tell them how to live their lives.

"Will they acquire horses?" Egon asked. "Those that might pursue?"

"It is my fervent hope that they do not," Cletus replied. "At least not until we have something of a lead upon them, at least. It is but a hard day's ride to Harhn from Teregossa. However, they will in turn be particularly ill-served if they choose to carry horses across the river."

"Why is that?" Ilvash asked.

"Horseflesh is prized by many predators in those places," Cletus answered. "The scent alone would draw them like flies. That is why we will find alternatives."

"Oh?" Egon spoke up.

He had not worried overly about such things, once he had spent enough time around the Puck to find the genial and jovial man honest and upright in his dealings.

A merry man, as such things went, infecting others with happiness like a song.

"At some distance ahead of us, we will meet a man," Cletus said more ominously. "I have previously hired his services and found him altogether reputable, however surly and antagonistic he might be perceived by others. That much is an act whose nature I have penetrated from time to time."

Egon nodded and returned his attention to the road before them. The sky in the east was brightening, promising a gloriously pleasant walk, rather than the rains that accompanied him south.

"And this man?" Ilvash asked. "What will he do?"

"Transport us in his wagon to Harhn," Cletus said with a smile in his voice. "And then accompany us into the *darkwilds*, where we will find his skills and experience most helpful."

"Wagon?" she asked. "What is it pulled by, then, if not a horse? No other creature will be faster. Certainly not an ox."

"Ah, you shall see," Cletus laughed. "You shall indeed see."

Egon kept his mouth shut. Goddess only knew what silly practical joke the Puck might have planned next.

At least it would be entertaining.

MID-MORNING. Past the farms and into places where pastureland and woods began to interlace. Cattle country, Egon would have called it back home, assuming aurochs with wide, sharp horns and pigs verging over onto feral in the woods.

Egon would have also called it bandit country, except that there was so little trade passing through here and farmers had almost nothing worth stealing. Egon assumed that these people around them mostly existed as a buffer against fell creatures crossing the mountains to emerge, rather than the river.

The road now was less of a road and more of a stretch of broken gravel. Egon could see where some high and mighty enchanter had once laid down a strip of stone as a roadway, but time and elements had broken it down and covered it with sand and dirt in places. Not much would grow, but nobody kept it up except for soldiers marching out to the Harhn to protect the keep and the few merchants making their way back and forth.

He became aware of a smell he could not place. Flatulent, but more like the woolly mammoths that northern kings occasionally rode. A big beast digesting grass.

"Cletus," he started to speak, but the Puck turned and smiled.

"Noticed her, did you?" he asked.

Her?

"We're quite close now, and the wind has shifted around," Cletus continued. He turned and pointed to a copse of trees a little off the road, perhaps a quarter mile away. "There, I presume. I asked him to join us about this far out."

Him?

Egon would have been concerned, but Cletus did not seem even slightly alarmed, so they must have finally caught up with their fourth member. Just because, he turned in place to look back up the road behind them. The land wasn't all that flat, so he could only see perhaps a mile behind them, and not even all of that as it dipped and rolled, but nobody had been up so early.

Horses would make up that space quickly, if the rider wanted, but they would also make a tremendous racket doing so. Egon just had to hope that the Dwarf didn't have anything like a flying carpet at his command.

"Come, come," Cletus chortled and picked up his pace some.

Ilvash hadn't been grumbling that much about the walk, and Egon had trudged many leagues overland, so he was used to it and had good boots.

As they got close, a figure emerged from the trees. Human in size and breadth. Male from the look of a gray beard kept reasonably trimmed. Egon still shaved every morning, but his beard was still coming in scraggly anyway. He'd have to be closer to thirty before it filled out impressively.

Like Ilvash, the fellow wore leathers, but his had the look

of real armor, boiled properly in oil and studded with rivets painted black against a dark green background.

"Well met, indeed," Cletus called out as the man stood by the side of the road, watching them approach.

That covered the him, but Egon had not yet discovered the her, so he kept his eyes open and roaming. And nose.

"Ilvash Marrove and Egon the Bold, allow me the indisputable pleasure of introducing you to Anders Wilson." Cletus positively beamed at them all. Anders studied them, but made no move to share hands.

Egon was not insulted. Southern clime. Southern culture. He did nod to the man, who nodded in return.

"Anders, my companions on this quest," Cletus continued.

"You being followed?" Anders spoke up now. It was a gruff voice, not used to salon company.

"Most assuredly," Cletus replied. "But we departed at false dawn, having bribed the guards to open the gates a wee bit early. None have threatened to overtake us on this road so far today, though we have been prepared."

"Best be moving on, then," Anders spoke in a tone that just seemed to be a grunt that came out in many syllables.

He reached into a pouch on his belt and pulled out a roll of what turned out to be off-white strips of rough cloth. Approaching finally, he handed one each to Egon and Ilvash.

"Tie this around a wrist or maybe your neck," he instructed them. "Jojo will know the smell for now, and by the time it fades she'll also know you by your scent as well."

Egon added it to the outside of his right gauntlet, puzzled but willing to follow instructions. He was interested, however, in why Cletus did not need such a thing. Did Jojo, whoever she was, already know the Puck?

"Come along," Anders grunted at them and led the

group back to a spot that had been hollowed out of the center of the trees.

It would be a perfect place for bandits to hide. Or for one to hide from bandits, perhaps.

There was a wagon in the center of the space, but Egon's eyes were drawn to the unicorn in front of the wagon.

He supposed you would call it a unicorn. It had one massive horn emerging from a spot midway up the long snout, but the base of the horn was thicker than Egon's thigh.

"This is Jojo," Anders said unnecessarily. "She's mostly tame, but don't let her step on your foot, and don't try to scratch her behind the ears for a few days while she gets to knowin' you."

Jojo was as tall as any horse Egon had ever met, but more than twice as wide and covered with a much thicker fur. Intelligent eyes followed him as he moved, so Egon held out the hand with the strip of cloth.

Jojo sniffed at warily and then snorted. Or sneezed. Something, as she ignored him at that point, sniffed Ilvash once, and went back to grazing from a pile of hay at her feet.

"Rhinoceros," Egon finally blurted out, recognizing the creature, or at least something similar.

"Indeed, Sir Orc," Cletus said. "A close cousin of the creatures from the far southern plains, having adapted themselves to colder, wetter climes and the more dangerous folk one might encounter."

Egon stepped back now and took the whole creature in. She was a rhinoceros, but even bigger than the things Egon had seen in his books back home. The sort of creature that might find a home in the cold north, if they were of a mind, although a whole herd of such beasts would be an interesting thing.

And Anders had tamed it enough to use pulling a wagon? Impressive.

"Mount up," Anders said, gesturing to the back of the wagon, where a canvas had been strung as a kind of tent.

Egon helped Ilvash off with her pack, and then put both in after she climbed inside. Cletus rode up front next to the Human, and the wagon lurched into motion.

It did not take long to reach the road itself, and then Egon was surprised at how quickly Jojo was pulling the wagon. He looked around the rear and noted a wide variety of barrels, from small ones holding perhaps a gallon up to monsters he might use as a tub, were he to cut one lengthwise.

Several hides were stretched on racks to dry, but Egon could not detect hardly any smell emanating from them. In fact, the whole wagon seemed to have almost no scent, which was odd, because when he put his nose close to a few of the barrels, the ripe sourness was almost overwhelming.

Who was this mysterious figure? Obviously a friend of Cletus, such that Jojo knew him on sight and smell. And apparently someone who would cross the river with them after Harhn.

Egon refrained from opening some of the chests he found, overriding his curiosity with the manners of a good guest.

He settled at the rear of the wagon, shaded yet, and kept watch on the road behind.

The Dwarf and his friends would be coming after them. That much was certain.

APPARENTLY, Jojo could outpace a horse, even while pulling a wagon. Egon was amazed when they reached Harhn as the sun was close to setting behind them. The road at least had gotten better as they approached, but there were few farms, and most of those gave the impression of pocket keeps. Not necessarily towers, but stout stonework with no windows on the ground floor save arrow slits.

They entered through a gate at Harhn and Egon found himself inside a large castle, except that it had an oversized tower on one side, and walls all the way around. As they stopped, he measured the courtyard against what he had known in the north, and rated it perhaps a half mile north to south and a quarter mile wide, with thirty-foot siege walls all the way around, but not many towers other than the keep itself.

The earth underfoot was hard-packed, though still gravel, rather than pavers. The inside had a large open space, that quickly gave over to narrow lanes that seemed to wind strangely, as though the city had been here first, and the walls only added later. Perhaps one of the more powerful wizards had raised them?

The Slayer Wars had drawn in any number of enchanters and powerful beings, all sides fighting one another, so Egon could see this outpost being a useful watchtower town on the old north-south road, out beyond what had once been the Gillanish Empire. Or perhaps this had been the edge. Egon didn't remember his maps and had not brought any with him, as they were all centuries out of date anyway.

A man emerged from the building next to the wagon and grunted. He and Anders carried on a quick conversation in a tongue Egon didn't speak, and then Cletus was leading them into the building where the man had emerged.

It turned out to be an inn with a common room. A low fire in one corner provided light, but the room was already warm, and several dozen folk sat at tables or a long bar, drinking and talking, mostly ignoring the strangers.

Those would be the locals, then. The people who lived in Harhn, as opposed to the mercenaries and troublemakers that came through to try their luck in the *darkwilds*. One last moment of light, before entering the darkness.

It was a morbid way to consider it, but Egon figured he should be honest with himself. He knew what slim percentage of people actually emerged from such a place with anything more than their lives. And how many never returned at all.

But Cletus had a map. And an enchanter in Ilvash who seemed to know her arcane lore.

And a cleric answering the call of the Goddess. It would be sufficient, though he wasn't sure how yet.

Anders joined them a few moments later, still looking curmudgeonly, but warming as they ordered food and beer and settled at a table rather away from the locals.

"My most profound apologies for brusqueness earlier," Cletus began. "We could have sat and chatted amiably, but I feared being overtaken on the road, so we pressed on, not even stopping for a proper break in the afternoon. We were, however, close enough to be able to rest here tonight, and again, breaking fast early and be on our way."

Anders nodded and grinned.

"What he's trying to say is that we're safe now, but figure that fool Dwarf is not far away," Anders said in a much more pleasant voice. He turned his attention to Egon now. "Servant of Brese?"

"Called," Egon replied, marking him as something more than just a follower.

"Oh?" Anders asked.

"Indeed, my old friend," Cletus spoke up. "A cleric, no less, blessed by the Goddess herself with power."

Egon didn't blush very often, but the meeting with that merchant's wife yesterday had disrupted his equilibrium, and he had not sorted himself out again.

"And you, mistress?" Anders turned to Ilvash now.

"Enchanter," she replied simply.

"Oh, more than a mere arcanist," Cletus said, turning to Anders. "She is the daughter of Merridee Marrove. And Thomas."

Anders' eyebrows went up in surprise, so Egon figured he should also be suitably impressed, even though the names meant nothing to him. He smiled, just in case.

"So stay here tonight and across the way on the morrow?" Egon asked.

"There are a few boats further south," Anders said. "But Jojo can also pull us across a nearby ford I know. The wagon was designed to float like a boat as necessary, and the water is well down right now."

A barmaid delivered a large pot of stew and several bowls, returning a few moments later with cups and a pitcher of a nut-brown beer that seemed far more malted than was usual down here in the south, where they seemed to think that hops were an essential food group.

Egon dug in last, after everyone else had filled their bowls. He said a quick, quiet blessing over his, not wishing to offend the others by suggesting anything.

"Perhaps we should invoke her protections," Cletus spoke up. "I would not with to give the lady offense otherwise."

Egon blinked at the Puck, but nodded and drew his hammer and held it over the center of the table.

"Goddess, please watch over this company and our friends," he prayed now. "Guide us to the light when darkness threatens and help us remember that justice still exists in the world."

"Amen," the others murmured and dug in.

They ate.

"What will we find in the *darkwilds*?" Egon asked between bites.

"The closer terrain is almost tamed," Anders replied.

"Many explorers and adventurers have cleared out vast swathes of it to the point that bold colonists could build there, were they of a mind, but the lands on this side of the river are still safer, and the population thin. It will be another century of peace before enough children are born to truly wish to cross over and live."

"But they could?" Ilvash asked.

"Indeed," Cletus spoke up. "The land within ten leagues of the river is almost civilized, but it gets progressively worse, the deeper one goes in. The closer you get to the old imperial capital at Gillanish. Those ruins are dangerous, because so much magic was used in the final battles that it permanently soured the land itself, only slowly leeching out, and then grounding into all manner of wildlife that has grown dangerous and powerful as a result."

"But it could be tamed?" Egon turned to Cletus.

"It could," the Puck agreed. "What vision drives you now?"

"I lack the knowledge, but there are elders I have known," Egon said. "They have been able to invoke the blessing of the Goddess to raise stout stone walls. I had wondered when we arrived if Harhn had been a village enclosed later. But if the lands could be tamed, outputs could be raised to push the evil and the monsters back…"

"That would require an army, lad," Anders said. "Well intentioned, but too expensive for Teregossa or any of the kingdoms further south. Right now, folks like me are the few willing to go in, not counting mercenaries and adventurers."

"And what do you do, Anders?" Ilvash asked.

"I am a Tallowmaster, Madam Marrove," he smiled. "Once, I was a mere candlemaker, a guild master in the city of Teregossa itself, working in a shop, but I grew restless."

"Restless," she repeated.

To Egon, it didn't contain a sarcastic note, nor a derisive one, so much as a prompt.

"Enchanters such as yourself often need exotic materials, frequently harvested from strange or magical creatures," Anders nodded. "I set out to acquire better materials than the average adventurer would bring me, because they have no idea what I might need."

"I noticed the hides in the cart," Egon interjected. "But none of them smelled."

"Aye," Anders chuckled. "After I take a beast, I skin it and strip the tallow, rendering it down, but I also know which herbs to mix in as I got in order to neutralize the smell. My candles are frequently worth four times my competitors, because they just render the fat down and call it good. Not everything has to smell bad. They just cut too many corners in my opinion."

"So you have training as a scout?" Egon asked, curious now.

"Of a sort, Sir Orc," Anders nodded. "I move through the *darkwilds* quietly, stalking my prey and either trapping it or hunting it. All such creatures can be harvested effectively when one knows those arts, so I sell bone to various crafter guilds, hides to the leatherworkers, tallow and candles to my own guild, and exotic ingredients to folks like Lady Marrove here."

"And he knows the quiet, perhaps secret ways to get us through the *darkwilds* without encountering brigands or monsters, that we might get close to our treasure without having to fight every step of the way," Cletus smiled now. "That will be important with Vorlothe and his friends on our trail. They might have a memory of the map, but not the thing itself, so they must either decide to chase us direct, wary now of whatever ambush we might lay for them, or try to instead circle around us and strike for the ruins directly, hoping that nothing scribed on the map might prove critical."

"Will the evil of the blade call a Harridan down to itself?" Egon asked quietly.

Cletus paused, pensive.

"That is indeed a wonderfully cogent question, Egon the Bold," he replied. "I cannot answer it. Perhaps you might ask the Goddess and see if she is willing to give you a sign?"

"I can try," Egon stammered after a moment.

Really, he was barely more of a journeyman as a priest than Ilvash as an enchanter, but his mind kept flitting back to that woman in the marketplace. Her words, even her presence.

Was the Goddess tracking this quest? Was it *that* important to the world?

He had no answer, so he ate.

MORNING THREATENED, but had not joined them yet as Egon rode in the back of the wagon again, next to Ilvash but watching the rear, with Cletus and Anders up front. Jojo apparently knew the way, or her eyes were even better than an Orc's in the darkness, because she pulled the wagon at a speed greater than he might be willing to run.

Egon had indeed been up extra early, that he might pray with a clear head. He had posed the question in his prayers, but received no answer. Not that he had expected to, as nothing on this quest had made sense on the surface of things.

He heard water flowing now. Not rushing, though still louder than the breeze that had been flapping the sheets of the wagon from time to time. He turned to look through the forward gap to see the river itself.

The sun was just rising now, bathing the land in red and gold. The river bed was wide, but low, cut into a variety of channels, where in the spring and summer Egon could tell that it would be nearly a quarter mile across. They hadn't been following a road, so much as perhaps an ancient path kept pounded down by Jojo's broad feet, among others.

They rumbled down a bank, jouncing much harder now as she pulled them over rocks and then began to spray water everywhere as she crossed the first of the many streams the river had been cut into by time. Egon and Ilvash both held on, and all the hides and barrels had been expertly tied down by Anders, so nothing moved around and they were able to stay put.

Then they were floating. It was an odd feeling to suddenly be in a boat, being tugged forward by a narwhal and skipping across shallows. Jojo did not seem to hesitate. Egon supposed that she had passed this way many times, if Anders hunted across the river. She would remember, as he had mentioned that she was at least as bright as a horse.

And friendlier, having sniffed him again this morning and then butting his outstretched hand for scritches.

It took time, but they made it across. The sudden quiet was almost unnerving, given the ruckus of the crossing. The wagon rolled to a sudden halt and both Anders and Cletus hopped off. Egon joined them, and then reached up and lifted Ilvash out as well.

The other men were kneeling by the side of the wagon, so Egon did the same. He was unsure what he was looking at, but they were making low and uncomfortable noises.

"Can it be fixed?" Cletus asked.

"Without doubt," Anders replied. "However, it will cost us perhaps half a day, unloading the wagon and then reloading it. I had hoped to get a greater distance away."

"What happened?" Egon asked, willing to show his ignorance here.

Mother and Father had both always said that a wise leader does not always have every answer, but must listen. They may still decide, but hearing all sides first keeps one from error.

"Cracked a spoke on the wheel," Anders said, reaching out a hand to touch it. "Best to fix it now before it shatters, but that will cost us."

"Is it just cracked?" Ilvash suddenly appeared, almost in Egon's shadow.

"Possibly," Anders shrugged. "Won't know until I get it out of the wheel, but I'll need to replace it from a spare anyway."

"Not necessarily," she replied, reaching out a hand and touching the same spot.

Egon watched golden light flow down the woman's arm and into the wood, illuminating the entire spoke for a moment before it began to soak in. A moment later, the golden fire emerged again and raced once around the entire wheel, lighting up every spoke.

Egon whistled. Ilvash looked up at him and blushed.

"The elders set you on many tasks," she smiled now. "Cleaning things. Repairing others. Some of it is makework, to teach a student patience, but a good chunk of it also grounds you into a whole set of spells and summonings that have use in everyday life. I know a conjuration that I can set to cleaning dishes or sweeping a room, so that I don't ever have to."

"Was it sufficient, master scout?" Cletus asked.

Anders ran his hand slowly over the wood and made a similar whistle.

"Better than it was," he said. "I might ask at a rest if you could touch the other three, Mistress, just to give us that much greater of an advantage in our travels."

"I would be happy to," she said, setting to work.

Quickly, they rose again and boarded the wagon, everyone smiling now. Jojo seemed to feel it as well, because shortly she was moving at a speed a horse might shy at. And pulling a wagon behind her.

Egon found himself looking forward to further adventure.

<hr/>

MID-DAY. They had crossed many miles and exited the valley that held the river. Egon found himself on a small outcropping of rock, looking back.

They had taken a longer rest to eat. Ilvash was touching the cart wheels and checking them all against her work. Cletus was smoking a cob pipe. Anders was pulling hay from a chest to supplement the grass that Jojo was pulling up with her enormous lips.

The land had risen, several soft ripples of hills, so Egon could only see the river in a few spots, and then mostly as a hint of blue on the horizon. Any riders that might be pursuing them were either invisible with distance, or hidden by terrain.

So they were alone.

Egon smiled and drew a deep breath into his lungs, letting the scent of the *darkwilds* fill him with wonder and excitement.

But something wasn't right. A tang in the air that didn't belong.

Off to his left, a raptor of some sort suddenly took flight with a raucous cry of surprise.

Egon shook his head and hopped off the rock, landing close to the wagon, where he reached in and located his shield, still attached loosely to his backpack. He pulled it into the open and strapped it onto his arm, turning right and left as he sniffed.

Ilvash looked up at him and frowned. Cletus rested his pipe on the ground nearby where it would not fall over. Anders studied him for a moment and reached for a crossbow he kept by his feet when driving.

Nobody spoke.

Egon circled the front of the wagon, noting that Jojo was apprehensive as well, stomping her feet suddenly, but not doing more than shifting her tremendous horn one way and then the other.

Egon drew his hammer and faced the depth of the trees where the meadow gave way. Something moved.

Correction, it charged.

Egon had a glimpse of an enormous beast, barreling forward on four limbs awkwardly, and then it rose up to its full height on rear legs.

It might have been born a bear. Or its ancestors had.

The creature was manged in places, hair falling out in strange patterns. It was nine feet tall and probably weighed double what Egon did. They stared at each other for a few, long moments, the beast sniffing.

Finally, it howled in rage and swiped at Egon's shield with a paw bigger than a dinner plate.

The blow staggered him backwards and to one side almost two steps. His shield rang like a bell and his arm was tingling as though asleep.

Rather than wrestle with the thing, Egon cursed it, invoking Brese's guile as a war goddess rather than relying on the brute strength of her brother Allowin.

A faint blue cloak seemed to descend on the creature, clouding its eyes and engulfing its hands.

The beast stepped forward and slashed again, but Egon was able to sidestep the blow. Similarly, it snapped at his with yellow teeth that crunched nearly a foot above his head.

A sound reverberated from Egon's left and a crossbow bolt buried itself in the monster's leg, provoking a howl of pain rather than rage. The bear turned to focus on Anders, and Egon shoved at it with his shield.

"No!" he snarled. "Here! Me!"

He swung his hammer, flat side forward and heard it crunch bone on the other leg. Perhaps they could lame the beast and evade it, because it had a look of rabid madness in those eyes. Except that the bear was wounded now, so it would be a danger to anyone it encountered.

The bear turned back to him and again swung. Egon's shield took some of the blow. His shoulder piece and vambrace prevented him from being gutted. He was able to snap his shield up into the thing's jaw as it tried to bite his face, possibly knocking a tooth loose.

A bolt of light exploded on the creature's chest, staggering it back almost a step and distracting it enough that Egon snapped his hammer into the same spot before it recovered. He stepped up and hit it again a third time.

There was no technique here. None of the dancing on the fighting floor than had been pounded into him by his father and older brothers first, and the warpriests of Brese later.

This was just a brutal match of strength against strength, but he had the armor to resist those claws, and the others did not. Egon would need to center the bear on him, lest it fall on someone those terrible claws could shred.

"Fear me!" he yelled in the giant's face as he swung again, connecting with an arm. "Flee me!"

Egon doubted that the beast understood anything, but it howled back and swung again. The curse held, though, as the blow went high and bit clear off to one side blindly.

Another bolt of light. A crossbow bolt missed, burying itself in the dirt.

Egon heard a quiet chanting that seemed to drill itself directly into his soul, but the bear was getting it much worse. Rather than attack again, it leaned back and howled its pain and fury at the sun overhead.

Egon took this moment to call down Brese's wrath on the beast. A bolt of holy fire emerged from the sky and bathed the beast. The heat was enormous, but it was magical, not real, so he did not need to fear setting the nearby grass aflame.

Still, it was sufficient. The beast staggered, tottering to one side. One more magical bolt struck it, but Egon had already seen the light go out in its eyes. It collapsed in silence, not even breathing.

Egon was breathing loud enough and heavy enough for both of them. He went to a knee and dropped his shield to one side. The claws had not done much damage, but he feared the infection of evil magic that seemed to permeate the beast, so he held up his hammer and touched his wounded shoulder.

Brese's warming hearth fires played over his chest, cauterizing the wounds and leeching the poisons before they could set.

"Are you well, my boy?" Cletus appeared in front of him now, still shorter in spite of Egon kneeling.

"I will be," he replied. "But I will need a nap before I am ready to do something like that again."

"We shall make sure you get your rest," Cletus nodded.

They both turned to watch Anders approach the beast, crossbow ready to fire. It was dead. Egon considered saying something, but the man was much older and had been doing this for a long time apparently, so he might not trust the kill until he confirmed it. Egon would no begrudge him that.

"What is that thing?" Egon asked, grabbing his shield and rising now.

Cletus and Ilvash stepped closer, but remained on Egon's flanks.

Anders knelt and prodded, before nodding and putting his crossbow to the side to pull out a long skinning knife.

"We call them Gray Bears," the man said. "Once just dangerous brown bears, perhaps your size, before the magic gets into their bones and blood and taints them. If we had the time, I'd strip this down to all manner of useful ingredients, but we need to be moving on from here."

"Could we not take the corpse with us?" Ilvash asked.

"I cannot lift such a beast," Anders laughed, turning to her. "Could you?"

Instead of answering, she began chanting, so Egon turned sideways to watch. A golden disk like an enormous shield appeared and slid under the creature, lifting it fitfully into the air as everyone watched. It began to move, so Egon paced it to the wagon, pulling the back open.

Anders and Cletus followed with sounds of marvel.

It balked at rising enough to clear the back gate of the wagon, so Egon slipped his hammer into the ring and dropped his shield. Grasping the closest limb, he pulled and lifted, getting it over the ledge and then grabbing more fur. It took several tries, but he managed to get the beast into the wagon.

Ilvash went to her knees as the light blinked out, but that was an exhaustion similar to Egon's. They shared a smile. Magic always seemed wonderful. However, there was always a price to pay.

"And that, my dear Anders, is that," Cletus laughed. "We will be able to continue on, and you can prepare it later when we stop for the day."

"Had I not seen it with my own eyes, I would not have

believed it," the man replied seriously. "But we can make someone a wonderful cloak. The meat will be tainted, but the bones can be cleaned. Those and some organs will be quite potent ingredients. And we'll make some candles, as this beast was fattened up nicely for winter."

"Should we stop somewhere and rest a full day?" Cletus asked. "It will give us a chance to watch for riders."

"I will find us a spot to hide," Anders nodded. "Failing that, someplace easy to defend."

They mounted up again. Ilvash ended up squeezed in between the two up front, with Egon stretched out more or less atop the bear's corpse. The smell was horrible, but Anders had rubbed a liniment of some sort onto the fur, so it was much fainter than it had been.

He didn't think he'd be able to sleep, but the bumpy road was smooth enough.

His dreams were ugly, but faded quickly enough whenever he woke.

EGON LOOKED around the camp Anders had found for them after a hard afternoon's ride. In a bit of a bowl formed of a hill that almost looked like it had been scooped out, protecting them well on two sides and sheltering them from the winds.

They had emerged onto something of a plateau now, higher up from Harhn below. Just another shift in the world. They were in a wooded place, and a bowl, so Anders had allowed them a fire to keep warm and cook their dinner. However Egon was in no hurry to eat.

He had again assisted Ilvash in getting the dead bear out of the wagon, but it was much easier going down than up, and had been quick. She decided to take a quick nap when she was done, so curled up under a blanket. Cletus was sitting nearby right now, smoking his pipe and keeping a watch on their back trail, so Egon found a nearby rock and watched Anders slowly and carefully peel the bear's hide with a knife.

"Do we need to dig a pit for the meat and offal?" Egon asked quietly.

Anders looked up for a moment and seemed to be measuring him.

"It would be useful, lad, ifn you're willing," Anders replied.

The Human almost sounded surprised that Egon was volunteering. Egon rose and crossed to the wagon, pulling is shield from his back and putting it on the tail gate, along with this belt.

The armor would remain on. He had learned to sleep in it reasonably well while walking south. And things might come sniffing for dead bear in the night.

So Egon began to hollow out a spot where the bowl came down. That would be easier than going up. Anders had grabbed a barrel from the wagon and was cutting pieces of fat from the hide to dump in.

"So how does it all work?" Egon asked as he dug.

He'd been a prince. Granted, a third son unlikely to ever inherit anything, short of a catastrophe back home, but he'd never wanted for anything in his life. Even as an acolyte, the Temple had been well funded and sponsored by the crown.

Craftsmen had been largely absent, save for the outcome of their expertise.

"The hide is not that great," Anders replied as he worked. "A proper bear doesn't have all these bald patches. But the skin will work up to a good leather. I need to scrape off all the fat and such from the inside so it's clean. There is fat all over the place, especially around the kidneys, and you store that in a barrel for now. Tomorrow, since we're going to rest here a day, I'll stoke up a low fire and render the tallow down for storage. I'll also start drying some of the offal."

"So killing that bear was a good thing for you?" Egon asked, still shoveling his hole.

"Without anything else, what I'll make for that bear will break me even for this trip," Anders smiled.

"Is that why you're doing this?" Egon pressed. "Taking these risks?"

"No, that's only part of it, Egon," Anders replied. "Sure, I make a nice living at it, but it's a task that needs doing."

"Needs?" he squinted.

"Like you said earlier," Anders nodded. "This land could be reclaimed, but it has to be cleared of all the bad things. This bear absorbed a host of bad magic from somewhere. Maybe what it ate. Maybe just where it slept. On the one hand, that magic is removed now from the soil. Sorcerers like Ilvash can use it in their work. One less monster roaming around hurting things. Maybe the land is a little purer. What about you? What brings you on this quest?"

"Something similar," Egon said. "The Goddess seemed to guide me to Teregossa, where I ran into Cletus. He has a need of someone like me, to help him clean the land and destroy certain things that might be used for evil. So, like you, I'll be reclaiming the land and making it better, that perhaps someday people can rebuild places like Gillanish."

"That's your calling?" the man asked. "Saving the world?"

"I don't know that I'd go that far," Egon grimaced. "But we must each of us strive. The Goddess teaches us to build, but it is also important to use our gifts to destroy, as long as we do so in a contained, prepared manner. Unmaking relics that can be used for evil. Or in your case, taking all that bad magic contained in the bear and turning it into useful things."

"Would you build fortresses to reclaim the land here?" Anders asked.

"I'd build villages," Egon decided. "But they must be protected, so that means towers as a bulwark, so I suppose everything we do here to defeat the evil that has been left to roam will help."

Cletus had moved close while they been talking, but he'd remained silent until now, just puffing contentedly on his pipe.

"And you, Egon The Bold," the Puck finally asked. "Will you be that bulwark?"

"I have my hammer and my shield," he nodded, even as he held a shovel and started digging a pit to contain rancid bear flesh. It was a task that needed doing, and he was best suited of the group. "I will stand."

Cletus and Anders shared a nod and a smile.

"And that, lad, is why a tallowmaster like me needs you here," Anders said.

Egon nodded in turn. The craftmasters needed the warriors protecting them from the things that would rend and destroy.

He would stand as long as he could, protecting them.

FOUR

NIGHT SOUNDS

EGON HAD SPENT years in the temple complex as a student, up late praying and then up again early to heat the forges for the masters. Such effort had made it easy to learn to sleep in his armor, and to suffice with odd catnaps during the day in the back of the wagon.

It was not his watch, but it felt like he had only just laid down. Anders had tapped his foot with a quiet nudge to rouse him without looking down. The man was watching something in the distance beyond their little bowl. Cletus was awake, but the slightest scent of anything seemed to be enough with the Puck.

Egon reached for his hammer before he was fully awake. His shield was nearby, though he had no idea what had happened.

It had been sufficient earlier to ask the Goddess for a blessing on their encampment. That was the sort of thing Egon always did in the evening, though since they had crossed into the *darkwilds* he had been more intent on using actual magic in such a way as to protect his friends.

He could see a line of faint red, a circle large enough to

contain all of them, the wagon, and the enormous rhinoceros unicorn Jojo. She seemed to smell something, as she had stood up from the way she normally slept kneeling, and one paw scraped at the dirt like she was preparing to charge.

To a bard, one might describe her as a horse with a horn in the center of her snout, though she was half again as tall, half again as long, and three times as wide. One did not bother herds of such creatures on the northwestern steppes, although Egon could only imagine what predators from that land might look like.

Egon looked beyond the circle he had scribed with the Goddess's help, in the direction that both Anders and Cletus were watching, then turned and looked the other way just because he had spent too much time dealing with common brigands.

Nothing behind them. He sniffed with magical senses as well.

Egon grabbed his shield and rose.

Eyes.

Watching from the darkness, but not the kind that presaged a pack of wolves or anything.

No, these had a golden fire to them, and they moved wrong. Egon held up his hammer and invoked the power of the Goddess.

Harridan. Oathsworn. He recognized the magical scent of Vorlothe The Dwarf out there, but it was not the man. He had apparently asked Ganchette the Stygian for some sort of arcane eye with which to seek his foes. His prey.

The Dwarf could not detect them at this distance. Still, he seemed to know where to look. Egon had never doubted the ones tracking them. Cletus had a map he had liberated from the evil hands of that Oathsworn, after all. And somewhere before them, supposedly enough that the very gods had stirred, waited the shade of Arinwa Hollenc, unholy champion and bearer of the blade *Ediade*.

Egon considered how the goddess's magic might aid him in hiding them from the Dwarf, then wondered if that very thing, the surge of protective power, was what the harridan sought. Bring Egon out in to the open for a battle on the aetherial plane, as it were, where Egon's power would shine like a beacon for bandits and magical monsters to see.

He turned to Anders and Cletus with a quick nod, then stealthed over to where Ilvash slept. They'd normally let her rest, but tonight, he had need of her arcane wisdom.

Like Anders, Egon tapped her on the foot, lest she come up with a spell on her lips. One pretty, Human eye opened and focused on him as Egon held a finger to his lips. She nodded and rose.

Ilvash also slept in her armor. Unlike his, hers was entirely decorative, soft leathers with a few rivets designed to make her look like a scout instead of an enchanter. It didn't reduce her power one bit. At the same time, any protective qualities were probably accidental.

Egon slipped close as she sat up and knelt beside her, one heavy, Orcy paw pointing into the middle distance.

"Vorlothe," he whispered in her ear. "How might we mislead him without a direct confrontation?"

She turned to look up at his smile, innocence which even included his tusks tonight.

"Mislead?" she whispered back.

"He cannot see us, because the Goddess has shrouded his eyes," Egon said. "Even the Stygian cannot pierce that, at least at this range."

"What would you suggest?" she asked.

Egon was at a loss. He'd had the idea, but not the image.

Anders and Cletus both slipped close now.

"Could you conjure or summon a dire polecat?" Anders asked in a low voice.

Egon understood both words, though polecat took him a moment. Skunks weren't native to the north where he came from, but wolverines were, and those were a foul-tempered cousin without any range to their musk.

Dire suggested largeness. Egon shuddered at the thought of a skunk the size of a wolfhound or larger.

Cletus's eyes lit up, and Ilvash joined him a moment later.

"Yes," she breathed.

Egon stepped back as the woman scrambled for her belt and pulled a few pouches open to grab ingredients. He went back to watching, but the eyes of Vorlothe just wandered along the nearby roadway, blinded by a deeper darkness than mere night.

Ilvash joined him a moment later, hands making esoteric passes as weird syllables came from her mouth. He spoke seven languages and read four of them, but didn't recognize what she was saying, other than it was power itself.

He added a brief prayer to the Goddess that her shroud would continue to mask them. No worthwhile forge cleric charges into battle like a berserker, after all. The forge teaches you patience in your crafting. A thing broken might be repairable, but better it not be broken in the first place.

Just as none of Vorlothe's brigands or hirelings had yet ended up dead.

Egon didn't think his luck on that score would hold much longer, but every creature decides over breakfast which of many gods and paths he will serve.

Evil just meant that theirs would likely end sooner. Possibly at the ball-peen end of his hammer.

Ilvash's hands glowed a pretty fuchsia hue that turned into a small cloud, floating across the bowl and down to where the trees approached the ancient road they had been following.

Jojo smelled it first, stamping her foot once and farting enormously. But her smell paled next to that ripeness the breeze brought them.

Egon hoped that the breeze didn't shift. After the horrible smell from that bear, he could only imagine what the fell magics of this land would do to a skunk.

A thing emerged from the trees next. Anders chuckled as Egon swore beneath his breath. It was the size of a small horse, with a tail pointed straight up and tipped over like a divining rod as it centered in on the Dwarf's spirit and waddled forward. All four of them stood perfectly still as the two closed, dwarvish eyes curious at what magic they had detected, while the polecat seemed offended to be sharing the same plane of existence.

Then the skunk did something Egon had never seen. Instead of turning to point its tail at the Dwarf, if planted its front paws and did a handstand, slowly walking forward with the tail straight out.

Egon heard the spray of musk as the two got close and a cloud that was somehow bright green in spite of the darkness enveloped the eyes. Even from where he stood, it smelled like something that had been fished out of the bottom of an outhouse and left to rot in the sun for three days.

And this was just the edge of it. Vorlothe had gotten it in the face, metaphorically.

His eyes vanished like a candle blown out.

"Thank you," Ilvash called as the creature turned this direction, back on all fours.

It seemed to nod once and then waddled back into the trees.

Cletus broke out in gales of laughter, echoing across the bowl where they slept.

"And that, my dear friends, is exactly why I thought that this particular company would be well-matched on such an excursion and adventure," he said. "Thank you for being such rewarding traveling companions."

Ilvash seemed to blush even worse than Egon, for which he was grateful.

"He seemed to know the general location, Master Colville," Egon said. "Can he track us?"

"Aye," the Puck nodded. "There are only so many roads one might take to Gillanish, but that he was searching so assiduously tells me that he has perhaps just now crossed the river. Perhaps he is still in Harhn, plotting his revenge and not yet in the field, so he needed to know if he should wait there for our eventual return, or to seek after us with deliberation and alacrity."

"And?" Egon asked.

"Oh, I suspect our worthy nemesis is even now making plans to break his camp at dawn or even earlier, that he might fly in our footsteps," Cletus agreed. "All the more reason to rest well now, and not tarry later. Much more adventure awaits us yet ahead."

Egon nodded a moved back to where he'd been sleeping earlier. He could always nap in the back of the wagon, at least for a while.

When the hounds of evil caught up, Egon the Bold would be the one who saw them first.

FIVE

FORGOTTEN

EGON STOOD watch as they took a mid-afternoon break. Cletus and Anders had their heads together over the map nearby, while Ilvash offered occasional commentary. He wasn't from these lands, having only just made it as far south as Teregossa, across the river, so there was little Egon could contribute to the discussion of geography.

Better he lay in wait for whatever predators thought to stalk them out here.

Anders had agreed that they had crossed out of the lands where hearty villagers might decide to colonize by building up towers, though it might be a century before such a thing occurred. This was approaching the heart of the unnatural *darkwilds* that had risen when battles between mighty wizards, powerful champions, and a few gods had completely shattered the land itself and poisoned everything.

Even the water around here was not to be trusted, until Egon had a chance to work the Goddess's magic over it in purification. Nothing killed or harvested here could be eaten, but they had sufficient flour and vegetables to last them possibly through the winter itself. And Egon could always ask the Brese herself for aid in perhaps enchanting a bush to bear magical berries that could sustain them for a few days at a time.

Right now, he used his great height to stand atop a broken stump of stonework that might have been part of a watchtower six centuries ago, and turn slowly in place, watching all directions. They were on something of a rise here, a hill defending two valleys spread out ahead and behind them on the path Jojo had been dragging them.

Egon tried to envision these lands as being the warm heart of a thriving empire, with the squares of land he could see as fields that had once grown crops or grazing beasts.

Nothing remained, save bits of stone here and there that hadn't yet collapsed from age. There was a village down below this saddle, ahead of them. It had not fared well when an army had marched through, from the way buildings seemed to have been knocked down. Perhaps a dragon or a wizard had blasted it with magical fire. Something.

Blowing dirt had accumulated like drifts and never been shoveled away, so Egon knew that the land had died on some summer day, six centuries ago, on the way to Gillanish itself. He saw movement now. A flickering, rather than a body. Almost a ghost, but it was in the light of day.

"Master Wilson, a moment?" he called to the other group, interrupting them without taking his eyes off the spot.

They were nearly a mile away, so he couldn't begin to say what he had seen. He kept his eyes loked on place, certain he had seen *something*.

"Aye, lad?" Anders asked as he got close, the other two trailing just as one would expect with folks whose first instinct was the spell rather than the hammer.

"I am certain I saw movement in the village below," Egon said simply. "It's gone now, and I don't know what it was. Are we certain we need to continue down this road?"

Anders studied him for a long second.

"Spoken like a much older warrior, lad," he said with a smile. "Not every problem has to be settled head on. Unfortunately, that bridge on the far side of the village is the only way across yon river for more than a day's travel either direction, and the river tends to be too broad and swift to ford in many places, even for Jojo."

Egon grimaced. He'd been afraid of that. Perhaps whatever it was that lived there was smart enough to understand that the bridge funneled food into its mouth?

Three of them had crossbows, but Egon suspected that such weapons would do little against whatever it was. Likely, it would come down to magic and steel.

Still, it was one thing to ride into the various dangers they faced, and something else to know to prepare now. He turned to Cletus. As did the others.

"I agree with your various sentiments, and share your sorrow that it must come to this, but at the same time, perhaps we can take undo advantage of the situation," Cletus replied brightly.

"Oh?" Egon asked.

"Well, certainly something lives there," the Puck grinned. "All of us would be seen as snacks, but so to would our dear friends trailing behind us, were we to somehow find a way across said bridge and perhaps leave it so damaged that they were forced to stop in the middle of the village, lest they fall into the river. Or flee with some terrible something nipping at their heels as they did. As dread Egon here notes on occasion, we can approach this sidelong."

"Sidelong?" Ilvash asked.

"Indeed," Cletus laughed. "Let's you and I give some thought to illusion now, while Egon considers stonebreaking."

"Stonebreaking?" Egon asked.

"You are the master of the forge, are you not?" Cletus smiled up. "He who makes also learns how to unmake, if I understand your explanations. That bridge had forded the stream intact for a millennia, but I think that perhaps the act of ending it would assist our greater cause by trapping many of the fell things of the farther east on the wrong side for now, thus opening the way for this side to perhaps be sooner cleaned out and recivilized by our friends at Harhn and other spots."

It took Egon a few seconds to translate that. Cletus never used ten syllables to say something when forty would let him achieve a more flowery and impressive effect.

"I will need time to pray," he said simply.

"Excellent, my mighty warrior friend," Cletus said. "You and Ilvash should go prepare for our next encounter, while Anders and I work out a few things beyond."

Egon found himself back alone. He remained up on that highest point to look around, even as he began a slow round of silent prayers. Ilvash was sitting cross-legged next to the wagon, as Jojo occasionally leaned over and sniffed her hair like the world's largest kitty cat.

He had no idea what magics might suffice. His work was with steel and other metals, rather than stone, although he had cousins and kin who worked with such a material.

The ancients had built that bridge by linking multiple arches together, having deflected the water itself so they could get down to the bed and work. The arch would be perpendicular to the force of the water, but an engineer would probably have hired an enchanter of some sort to reinforce the mortar. Doubly so if it had outlived the empire for so many centuries.

He would need to introduce entropy to the mortar. Rot that would pull things apart and soften them, much like the heat of the forge caused metal to turn soft.

He thought of the seasons that had passed. Heat and cold cycles the bridge had endured. The pounding of ice coming down from the mountains and perhaps still heavy enough to hit like his hammer.

At the same time, it would not take much. The river continued to flow, pushing relentlessly against the one side and tugging at the other. Given a few days, he was certain he could do such a thing, but there was something living in the village, and other somethings on their trail, so he would need to strike with power, rather than the patient expertise of the steelshaper.

He would have to break a sword, rather than forging it.

Brese willing, he thought he had an idea how.

THEY APPROACHED the village on the only road. Crossing the overgrown and broken fields would only slow them down and let Vorlothe and his friends catch up with them. And the thing hiding inside the ruined village had not appeared again, but Egon sensed it as Ilvash and Cletus did, as well, but all of them were blessed with some level of magic.

Only Anders had to rely on eyes and ears that could be fooled, but Egon suspected that the Human had grown cannier than whatever beast lay hidden within the rubble.

Jojo was unhappy, turning right and left in her traces and snorting angrily, as if she could smell something, but not identify it.

Of course, right now she was magically masqued to look like a pretty Percheron, similar to one of the great horses Egon had learned to ride when he was younger. Big enough to bear the weight of a full-grown Orc with armor, but nowhere the size of her true, furry, rhinoceros self.

Likewise, Egon appeared as a simple man at arms, clad in a good chain and bearing a simple wooden shield. Cletus and Ilvash wore more the appearance of travelers than warriors or casters, but the hope was that the creature was either smart enough to make for the only warrior in the group, or stupid enough to make a play for the "horse."

Egon decided that he and Jojo could both hold their own long enough for the others.

As they rode, he invested a little of Brese's forge magic into his shield and his hammer. Not much, but enough to temper the steel better.

He didn't suppose that the creature who hunted these ruins and guarded this bridge would be amenable to simply letting them pass.

Jojo stopped moving now and planted both her back feet. The plan called for Anders to ride hell for leather across the bridge if they could distract the monster long enough, and then use that vantage to fire his crossbow while the others slowly retreated.

Only if Jojo would be willing to play.

Egon slid down from the side of the wagon when she seemed stubborn, and walked up on her left, his shield side, talking in soothing tones.

One angry eye flickered back to size him up and she snorted again.

"I'm here," he reminded her, uncertain how smart the rhinoceros was, but certain that it was greater than a horse.

Egon took a slow step forward, head on a swivel at half-fallen buildings and hammer ready to mash. Jojo seemed mollified that someone else would go first, as she started forward at the same walking pace he moved, wheels rumbling quietly on dirt-covered pavers half-buried by time.

Everything was the silence of the tomb, but he could feel eyes upon him.

In his hands, the hammer was illusioned to appear a simple sword, so he held it out in front of him like a lucky talisman, even as he pushed outward with a pulse of forge magic. Back home, it had been the sort of thing you forced down into the sword looking for flaws in the metal that needed to be hammered out again lest they broke in battle later.

Here, he was looking for that thing that stood out against the quiet serenity of the village itself.

There.

Something.

Egon sensed a dark hunger, rather than the sort of malevolent intent that Vorlothe gave off in person. That was good, as it suggested a monster rather than something intelligent and perhaps undead. He had no doubt such things yet lurked ahead, but if he could distract this one, they might get past and let Vorlothe deal with the thing instead.

Egon flinched and nearly screamed with surprise when a second version of him appeared, walking alongside. And then a third.

Then his mind caught up and he understood just what sorts of misdirections were about to occur. He pointed forward with his hammer and watched the copy of himself do the same.

Okay, that was an awesome distraction. He grinned and moved a little faster to get out ahead of Jojo.

Something growled, as if threatened. It suggested that the something over there wasn't sure if Egon was lunch or something to be avoided.

Egon changed the spell effect he had originally had in mind and shifted to something that might make three of him enough to stop someone from scrambling out of the ruined inn or greathouse ahead on the left, where the sound had originated.

Brese heard his call and Egon felt the world shrink around him. Except that they had stayed the same and he was more than twelve feet tall now. Wielding a hammer that looked like death itself, falling from the skies. Two more of him did the same.

He stomped a foot, just to make the sort of noise that one did when there were a thousand pounds of angry Orc involved. The muffled thump echoed off the faces of broken stone buildings as the road began to widen out into something that might have been a market square, once upon a time.

The thing inside charged.

Egon saw a green-gray lizard with six legs and a mouth like a crocodile rushing madly towards him. It began to glow, even as it crossed the space, like a certain Puck was painting it with his own magic.

Egon braced his feet at first, then stepped quickly to his right, flashing the shield at the thing's snout like a red cape to distract it.

As if three of him all doing the same thing wasn't enough distraction.

The blue fire surrounding the beast seemed to coalesce into a spot, so Egon smashed the thing right there with his hammer as it went by, suddenly turned back into an armored Orc, but also still large as long as he concentrated on the effect.

Twelve feet tall also meant much stronger, but he'd pay for it later. For now, he needed to invoke something like the power of the ancient giants anyway, so it had been close to the top of his mind.

All three of him seemed to strike at the same place, such was the power of the illusion Ilvash had cast. The lizard monster had leapt up to snatch at the shield, and Egon's blow drove it face-first into a wall that collapsed atop it in a puff of dust.

He pounced before the thing could dig itself out again as rocks fell, smashing it on the back with his hammer, even as a saw-toothed tail swiped him in the thigh. The bruise tomorrow would be enormous, but living to tomorrow to see it would be acceptable.

Jojo wanted to take a bite at it, but Anders yelled and cracked his reins at her, so she started moving. Maybe she was willing to let Egon handle the thing, if it got her to a nice spot to munch on some fresh clover. She could be like that.

Arcane bolts in red and gold slammed into the creature like rocks dropped into the mud and splashing. The beast thrashed, but that just seemed to bury it a little more.

"Egon, away now," Cletus yelled, so he backed three steps before turning the fleeing in the wake of the wagon.

Jojo was going like hell for the bridge, with Cletus and Ilvash standing in the bed and holding on to the siderails as Anders focused forward. More bolts from the two casters raced over his shoulders. Egon just needed to focus on the bridge. One foot in front of the other. Pounding, but so much faster because of his longer legs.

He even kept up with Jojo for this brief of a jaunt, his long legs helping cover ground. He glanced back and saw more Egons dancing with the lizard monster as it began to dig itself out, still in the square, giving him time.

Egon stopped in the middle of the bridge and considered the thing beneath his feet. Three arches, spanning a narrow spot in the river, with deep stone on both sides that had been cut by ages of water. Originally, he had planned to shatter the middle span, but the creature had short legs. It might not be able to launch itself from the near bank, so all he had to do was break the place where the bridge rested.

The wagon cleared the far end as the casters poured more energy into wounding and distracting the beast, so Egon took a breath and pushed that same detecting spell into the bones of the bridge itself. It had been effective at finding flaws in swords, but he had never considered the wider uses it could be put to until now.

Like finding monsters hiding out of their normal place. Or bridges that might be old.

It was like Egon suddenly had a second set of eyes watching the stone. His three companions could not see as deep into the darkness as Egon could, but this spell was more of magical sense that he might share with Cletus and Ilvash.

Planting his feet, he dropped now to one knee and swung his enchanted hammer into the stone of the bridge's surface. It rang like a bell, but that was the way his eyes and ears had been adjusted. To the others, it was probably a dull thump.

There. The upriver corner where the bridge attached to the land. The cracks were almost invisible today, such was the power of the enchanter who had worked this bridge so long ago, but they were there. Egon moved to that corner and struck at the corner pillar. The piling, he thought they were called.

A second blow. A third. Brick began to chip.

It would be easy to fall into the rhythm of the forge here, but counterproductive with that lizard still about. Egon looked up and saw it dancing with a version of Ilvash that seemed twenty feet tall, her hands licking out with something that looked like a scarf for the creature to bite at.

Weird, but it seemed to be doing the trick, keeping that thing over there.

He struck again, pushing some of Brese's power into the gap he could see now, like gold used to fill the gaps left when a treasured vase fell and was repaired by an artist. The stones began to glow softly, a filigree of light spreading slowly across this arch as he stepped across to the other piling.

Three blows here and the golden lines connected, a net now that spread from side to side.

Egon backed to the center of the first arch as the beast finally realized that it was fighting a ghost and turned his way. Bolts from behind him, eldritch and crossbow, began to rain on it as the thing shook its head a few times, as if clearing cobwebs.

It spotted him across the space and started forward, warily though, as though it had learned some misgivings. Egon smiled. That was a useful way to put it.

He swung one enormous blow overhand, dropping to a knee as he did for the extra power, and struck the spot that Brese had finally showed him, the exact center of this arch, where all the other stones pushed together into a single keystone, somewhere below him, that held this span in place.

It popped. Or perhaps turned to dust under his blow, because Egon felt the entire structure beneath his feet lurch and sway now. He scrambled backwards as the lizard started picking up speed, pushing at the remaining stones with his magic as he did.

There was a sound like cloth tearing, and the full width of that span of bridge collapsed into the river with a tremendous splash. Egon held his place nearer to this bank but still on the remaining stub of the bridge itself, in case the beast could indeed make such a jump. However, it had short legs, much like the crocodiles he had seen in books, and no wings with which to glide across.

Hopefully, it did not swim well, either, with such raging fury as it stopped on its side of the gap and howled at him in frustration.

But the beast stopped short, rather than trying to jump across the gap. Egon was still twelve feet tall, though there was only the one of him now. He could hold this bridge like one of the ancient heroes, at least long enough.

A long tail whipped side to side and more hisses and growls, but the thing did not try to leap that twenty-foot gap to get to him. Hopefully, it couldn't.

Egon backed slowly off the bridge as the creature settled. A gold bolt struck right in front of the thing's snout and it suddenly turned and raced for cover, hissing like a tea kettle as it did.

Egon let go the breath he had been holding and sagged. He even released that spell that made him a giant, and felt the crush of exhaustion land on his broad shoulders like he was trying to carry Jojo across the bridge.

"That, my boy, was a most excellent example of the value of misdirection and subtlety," Cletus spoke. "Perhaps the various gods who pay attention to such things will be mollified that we don't necessarily wade through the spilled blood of our foes on the way to wherever we are heading, and take pity at some later venture."

"One can hope," Egon gasped, staggering to his feet now with help from the side of the wagon.

"You rest," Anders said. "They can keep watch while Jojo and I get us deeper into the *darkwilds*. The map shows a place where that previous group once rested, just before entering the outskirts of the city itself, so we should be able to make it there today."

Egon nodded. A nap right now sounded like heaven. He couldn't remember putting that much effort into anything, even forging a new sword for the king for his birthday had been easy by comparison. Tossing his shield and hammer into the back, he curled into a small bundle and let the rattle of the cart rock him to sleep.

SIX

VISIONS

EGON DREAMED. At least he hoped it was merely a dream and not a portent of something darker. He stood in a vast hall, lit by rows of magical torches, hanging from arcade pillars, as two masses of Humans clashed, red and gold meeting gray and blue by the color patterns they wore to lace armor and their tunics.

He was a nameless soldier in this battle, but somehow close in to the captain that led the red and gold, though he did not know the man's name. The warrior bore a bastard sword that an Orc would have appreciated, and it glowed with a silver light brighter than mere steel.

Ahead of them, the gray and blue army held a dais and Egon somehow realized that this was the throne room itself for the Emperor of Gillanish. Atop the stone, a man stood out from the others, wielding a sword similar in size to the captain's, but glowing with a malignant red heat that seemed to draw the very warmth out of the room.

Champion of Darkness Arinwa Hollenc then, bearing the famous soul-taker *Ediade*. Outside, armies clashed and died in their multitudes, but they were only sound, even then barely audible above the clash of arms within. Red and gold surged into the gray/blue wall, men falling on both sides as two mighty heroes slew relentlessly.

Egon-as-ghost-warrior stayed close to his captain as the two champions finally fought through the morass to meet each other. Soldiers on both sides seemed to shrink back by some unspoken agreement now, letting those two men settle things.

Each blow seemed to fill the room with blinding light as the swords hacked and blocked. The sound was of titans forging worlds with hammers, inexorable and impossible to escape.

Arinwa slipped the captain's defenses after a time and *Ediade* struck, plunging through the man's mail armor and into his stomach. Egon and all his friends groaned in stunned disappointment as their champion was about to fall, but then the man did something Egon could not have imagined.

The captain reached out with a hand and grabbed that red blade with one hand, holding it place even as it was killing him and eating his soul. With the Champion of Darkness pinned down, the captain struck with his own sword, Arinwa's head toppling slowly backward off his neck as a spray of arterial blood fountained into the air.

Egon and his army surged forward in an invincible rage as the gray army watched stunned. They had lost their captain, but took their vengeance on the others, until the stones were slick with blood running into the drain.

EGON AWOKE with a hard start and a gasp.

"Better, lad?" Anders asked, seated nearby.

Egon looked up and saw stars overhead. He sat up suddenly and found himself stiff, looking all directions.

"Cletus thought it better to let you sleep," the man continued. "Ilvash got you off the wagon with her magic and we've kept watch over you all afternoon and evening. Stew?"

Egon discovered a bottomless hunger in his belly, similar perhaps to what *Ediade* had sung before dying. He nodded and Anders filled a bowl from the pot over the fire and handed it to him.

Egon worked on getting his heart rate and breathing back to normal. After chasing Jojo across the river, it felt like he had run here all the way from Teregossa in a day.

Cletus woke now from his meditations and ambled over. Rather than speak, he just studied one weary Orc for a long minute as Egon got some broth and meat into him.

"That was more than a mere dream," Cletus announced.

Egon fixed the Puck with a hard eye but kept eating, certain that as soon as he spoke the stew would turn cold before he got back to it. Ilvash had apparently been awake as well, as she sat up but remained a third of the way around the fire.

The empty bowl seemed to assuage some of the emptiness in his soul, so Egon grabbed his waterskin and emptied it as well. Brese would bless him with the power to refill it, if he was lucky, but Anders had also found them a stream or creek from the sound of babbling water close by.

"I stood in the throne room," Egon finally said. "On the day of the final battle, when Arinwa was killed. But I seem to remember that *Ediade* vanished, never to be seen again."

"It did, my boy," Cletus nodded sagely. "As did Arinwa. Rumor suggests that some dark power they had been attempting to summon had just enough power into this world to take them both and entomb them below, even as five armies, several dragons, and perhaps a demigod or three fought each other to be the first to lay hands on that blade."

"My captain had a silver blade," Egon said, struggling to

separate dream from reality now. "He fought Arinwa and held his own, until dying finally. But in that last moment, he struck Arinwa's neck clean through. Is that what happened?"

"Who knows?" Cletus answered in that singsong he did when he was tale-telling. "Nobody in that throne room that day made it out alive afterwards, according to the few survivors of the war itself. Perhaps Brese guides you with her memories?"

Egon shrugged.

"Do we know who the captain was?" he asked instead.

"I've heard no legends, Egon the Bold," the Puck nodded. "Describe who all you saw."

So Egon did, working from the moment he first appeared in the guise of a veteran on the front rank, clear to the ending of the vision. The stars overhead seemed colder and more remote by the time Egon was done talking, so Anders had added a pair of logs to the low fire, using the light and heat in an attempt to drive the cold back into the trees.

"Gold and red would have been the Kingdom of Karnegriand," Ilvash spoke up quietly when he finished. "Gray and blue was the Vyakin Clans of the east northeast, beyond Gillanish's farthest border. You're sure those were the colors?"

"I am," Egon said. "Is it important?"

"The Vyakin were wiped from history," she explained quietly. "Gone completely in that generation and never seen again. Karnegriand is the old name for the lands just to the south and west of the current Teregossa, that side of the river ranging perhaps as far as the mountains in their day. When they fell, it still took Teregossa nearly two centuries to turn into something else, on that spot where three trade roads intersected and hunters like Anders might try the lands beyond Harhn."

She turned to Cletus and Egon watched something pass between them. Confirmation of some rumor, perhaps?

She turned back to him now.

"Clean, silver blade in the captain's hands?" she said. "Magical white light when it met the red power of *Ediade*?"

"Yes," Egon said simply, still lost but aware that the woman was an arcane scholar of deep learning.

"That was the Crown Prince of Karnegriand, then," she said. "He was lost in the final battle, along with his entire elite Guard. That's who you were in that vision. Do orques believe in reincarnation?"

"We do not," he said simply. "You are born, given your chance to shine in the light of Brese, or Allowin, or perhaps one of the others, and then taken and judged for the whole of your lifetime."

Simple things that every child was taught. Grow up strong of will and loyal of heart, regardless of the flesh the binds you to the world. Always be the best you can, knowing that you will fail, but never letting depression color you into stopping when you might yet strive for one more step forward.

That he had been Called by the Goddess was her decision, that an idiot third prince had a greater value to the world on the road in worn leather boots and slightly battered armor, rather than home as a scholar of governance or literature.

"I don't know, without being able to consult my books, but a goddess very much like Brese was worshiped by Karnegriand in their time," Ilvash said. "Perhaps another facet of her power, or however they might explain it. To me, it sounds like she found a trooper in her army and sent his memories down to you. Otherwise, I might say you were a Human in a previous lifetime."

"I have better karma than that," he grinned at her.

She grinned back.

"So does that mean they might all be there still?" Egon asked. "All those fallen, both good and evil?"

"We shall see, Egon the Bold," Cletus nodded sternly. "We shall see."

SEVEN

EMPIRE

THE MAP HAD LED them true, as though it would have been hard to get lost when all the roads shown led to the ancient ruined city once known as Gillanish, from which an empire had sprung.

All empires fall. Such was the nature of things. Egon said a quick prayer for the shades of all those nameless and forgotten people who had never rated legends or books dedicated to their exploits.

It had been a tremendous city, once. Even now, the ruins stretched for miles in front of them from that last plain upon which Egon supposed armies had perished. He could see where walls had once stood, falling in on themselves in many places, breached in others. A few spots had giant sinkholes, as though the earth itself had opened beneath and dropped a section of the wall directly into hell.

Egon could smell the lingering scent of evil and destruction, six centuries hence, but he knew that it was in his mind, reacting to the immense magics that had been unleashed here.

Monstrous demons or elementals, giant-sized in scale,

had rampaged, kicking paths forward for armies to follow. Dragons had flown low enough to ignite even the stone with the power of their caustic breath.

Devastation.

And no one had returned to try to rebuild after the few survivors had limped home. No one have even tried, other than greedy adventurers, evil fools, and a few scholars intent on trying to cap that well of evil forever, if they could.

"Are we enough?" Egon looked over at Cletus, standing next to him as the four of them stood next to a hairy, farting unicorn and looked at the place.

"I believe so," Cletus replied, leaving it at that.

Such paucity of words told Egon how closely the Puck was holding his thoughts right now, to not spend a paragraph in explanation intended to buck everyone's feelings up.

A tallowmaster, a storytelling minstrel, an enchanter, and a priest, to face off against the darkness itself.

He turned and looked back over his shoulder. More than once, Vorlothe the Harridan had sent his power seeking after them, but the combined magics of the three had blocked such probes, and Ilvash was always ready to summon another polecat if things got close.

Egon could not tell where Dwarf and his party were, so he hoped that they were back there somewhere, hopefully weakened by that creature guarding the bridge, or delayed in working the long way around it.

"Master Wilson, what manner of creatures might we find in there?" Ilvash asked now.

"The meanest ones," Anders replied. "Those that drove out or ate the rest, so they will be smart, stubborn, and possibly infected with the demonic power everywhere."

"Undead?" Egon asked sharply.

Brese had given him a shard of her power specifically for such things.

Anders shrugged and nodded to Cletus.

"Undying, perhaps," the little man said. "Touched with death, but not drawn down into it. Possibly intelligent enough to worship it for power, much as our Dwarf friend does, so we should exercise even greater care at this point and assume that anything we meet might be a willing servant of darkness, rather than a mere wild creature born hungry, like our dear friend back at the bridge."

Egon grunted. He'd made it this far without having to splatter too many brains along the way, one idiot wanna-be necromancer notwithstanding. But he suspected that was all going to change soon.

The Goddess had called him south for a reason. And seemed to be watching over him along the way.

"If the thing entombed him, does the map show the way?" Egon asked.

He hadn't spent much time studying the map Cletus had acquired. He was really just here are muscle, after all. Let those three sort out the intricacies.

Personally, Egon wasn't sure that Vorlothe nor his friends might be literate enough to actually handle such a task, since cartography was usually a profession, rather than a mere hobby. Especially if you were intending to walk into dangerous caverns and ruins.

Anders pulled the map from an inner pocket of his jacket and unwrapped the oilskin protecting it. Egon watched him unfold the clean vellum to show this portion of it.

Gillanish as it had been, using an older map that was subsequently marked over with notations of pits, tunnels, and collapsed buildings. Whatever fell creatures lived here were taken as a given.

Egon could see the first bridge at the edge of town, a tributary where four like it all converged near the ancient center of the city and provided roadways for boats in nearly every direction. Almost no buildings survived this far out. Just a rolling field of rubble with a few, twisted trees and some stunted grass growing.

He wondered what it might have looked like if this city had been further south, where a jungle might have reclaimed some of this land and perhaps begun pulling down some of that evil magic as trees aged and died, but somehow it felt better to be semi-desiccated now. Shattered and abandoned.

He looked down at his feet just to see if there were any ants or bugs about. It was the lack of birds overhead that really got him. Egon was used to seeing all manner of hunters up there, gliding and calling, but the sky overhead was empty. Not even buzzards to feed on the dead.

At least until they roused whatever might eat smaller things and still be small enough itself to fly afterwards. He had his crossbow in the wagon, as did the others, just in case.

"Where do we leave Jojo?" Cletus asked now.

"I'd like to see if that one building on the right, about a ring in from the old wall, is stable," Anders replied. "It has the feeling of an ancient stables, so she might be comfortable there, and we can leave her food. I doubt much in here would be a threat to her, especially with us wandering around making noise."

They moved.

Egon noted how the roadways were often two or more feet buried with rubble and blown dirt at this point, so that he found it less painful to just walk out front, rather than ride in the bed. Ilvash joined him quickly, while the other two rode on the springed buckboard in a little comfort. Nothing here was sufficient to stop Jojo, but that didn't make it a pleasant ride.

And it put him on point, where he felt more at home. His shield between all his friends and whatever might threaten them. His hammer ready to smash evil down. Ilvash trailed a little, but close enough to see when he turned his head that way.

"What do you see?" he asked her at one point.

She started to retort, then thought about it.

"The number of deaths, and the magics involved, have turned it all into something like a fairy tale," she said. "If you could drain all the evil from the stone, you could built a magical fortress even an Elf would be proud to own with what remained, but the evil and the magic are too wrapped up in each other, so you'd have to pray over every brick."

Egon grunted. About what he suspected. And more work than he intended to do, but he could see someone forming a religious organization one of these days. Build a retreat nearby and have the penitent literally pick up a rock and spend a day purifying it, then selling it on to some enterprising nobleman.

The world was filled with people crazy enough to try.

He was following what looked to be a trail of some sort in the soil, packed down by generations of footprints, though he could not tell what they were.

"Master Wilson?" he called, pointing.

Anders stopped the wagon and hopped out, crossbow in hand as Jojo snorted and sniffed for things to eat.

"Wolves," he said after kneeling. "Big ones, too. Bigger than you get up north."

The mountainous cold made all wild animals larger, so that was an impressive size. Perhaps four feet at the shoulder for the biggest? He scanned the vicinity.

Jojo sniffed the trail now and stomped an angry foot. Anders moved to scratch her behind an ear and settle the beast.

"Does all this imply that said tracks were laid down recently?" Cletus asked.

"Last couple of days," Anders agreed, not taking his own

eyes off the horizon either. "They circled in from the north, I think, rather than coming up from behind us."

"Our old foe?" the Puck asked the universe, but nobody answered.

They made it quickly to the old building and confirmed that it had at one point been stables. The stone walls were more intact here—made sturdier—but the wood roof had long since fallen in and rotted into mulch and dust. Jojo got settled with protection from the wind and a huge pile of hay and grain to keep her settled. The wagon was parked in front, once it had been turned to make their departure easier.

"What happens to her if something happens to us?" Ilvash asked.

"She's smart," Anders said. "After a day or three, Jojo will start wandering, mostly to the creek and back to drink. If we're gone a week, I have a horn that she could hear up to a mile away that would call her. If it's longer than that, I suspect she'll be making her own way out of the *darkwilds*, lass."

"Oh."

Egon nodded. Smarter than a horse. Friendlier, too, although not as affectionate as a dog. Great big kitty in many ways.

Everyone loaded up their packs and fell into an order that saw Anders out front now and Egon at the back. Cletus and Ilvash walked side by side and he formed the base of a diamond where he could get up to the front quickly or cover both flanks from an attack.

From wolves, or whatever they were.

The bridge over the next riverbed was broken, but the water itself was low as fall weather settled. They were able to step off the marble sidewalks that still held largely intact and onto the rubble piles of another doomed bridge. Egon regretted breaking the first one, but it would make the lands better over the long run, if it kept monsters on this side for a time and let settlers tame the far parts.

The neighborhood on the far side of this river felt more upscale, like perhaps this river was the line separating merchants from the people who worked as menials and farmers. The buildings were no more intact, but they had been bigger once. A few still survived as jagged walls, like broken teeth in the air, but it just meant that the buildings might have trails around them where the dirt still grew occasional grass. Nothing Egon would eat, but it was useful to know where he might try some plant magic later.

"Did anyone escape the city before the siege?" he asked the others.

Southern history was something he was only tangentially cognizant of. Doubly so this far back and so many hundreds of miles from home.

"A few, Master Orc," Cletus replied. "The wise ones saw the rise of men like Arinwa Hollenc and raced to their country estates when his voice became the most prominent in the Emperor's ear, but the civil war had already begun to burn at that point, so the roads were no safer than the city. Many chose to withdraw to their palaces here, these fine buildings around us, and likely died in them."

"Would there be treasure within these ruins, if one managed to dig?" Egon asked, more from idle curiosity than anything. He didn't need much coin and rewards for evil-doers usually sufficed.

The others, however, might have greater dreams.

"Indeed so, Egon," Cletus said. "But the mere act of digging will attract the eyes of the fell denizens of this place, so we would be attacked quickly and to no end."

Egon nodded. That didn't suggest that they might not come back and maybe try a few of the more intact palaces later. Gold and silver would survive, even as artworks and fabrics would rot.

He would get an equal share with the others, but Egon wasn't sure what he would spend it on. Extending the walls around Harhn to enclose more space for merchants? Building a tower of some sort on the other side of the river, a mirror image to Harhn, so that settlers might be drawn to that side?

He supposed that if there was enough cash involved, he might found a militant order, dedicated to going into the *darkwilds* and removing some of the more dangerous predators. It wasn't like it would be his money at that point. Just loot recovered from lost souls and put to useful outcomes.

Gillanish had been huge when it died. Perhaps a million souls had lived in the vicinity, if the ancient stories were true. Enough that the original walls had been torn down and pushed out four times over the centuries, leaving ring roads of a sort and then not rebuilt at the end. Only the old imperial palace, up on its hill overlooking the ancient settlement, had real walls left.

Dragons didn't care. Nor did some of the more powerful enchanters or demigods. The four of them traveled all day forward and Egon watched those grand, stone walls come slowly into focus. They even looked intact, but for a few spots where it looked like a giant mouth had taken a bite out of them.

"How hollow is that hill?" Egon asked, studying it.

"Completely," Cletus laughed. "There was no hill originally, so some of the earliest wizards built a false-mound for the king's palace. Subsequent generations extended it up, down, and sideways, until the thing looked more like a ziggurat than a palace at the end. I have seen illustrations done when it was at its peak and covered nearly a square mile of ground."

"Huh," Egon grunted.

"Something amiss, my friend?" Cletus asked.

"Down suggests that they burrowed under the city," he said. "Water pipes and perhaps catacombs. Does the map show where previous groups. might have tried penetrating the palace from the side or bottom first, rather than fighting their way through whatever was dangerous enough to live in the old throne room?"

He caught knowing glances from the other three.

"They looked, but were unable to locate such places," Cletus said. "There were many valiant attempts, but the sewer systems had largely collapsed from earthquakes and time, blocking up every tunnel they entered."

"Did they have magic?" Egon asked.

"Not forge magic," Cletus grinned.

Of course. Wizards and enchanters built themselves magical eyes and ears to spy on people, perhaps summoned a creature into a mirror to show them scenes. They did not seek the points of entropy where a blade might be weak.

Or strong.

They would have needed a cleric of Brese or some similar god. Or whatever powers a demon might grant his favorite Harridan Dwarf. Egon suspected that Vorlothe might not be as crippled in his searching as most.

Why bother recruiting a broken tool, after all?

Egon wondered if the demon that propelled Vorlothe was the same one that had once raised up Arinwa Hollenc to power and glory. Up until now, it had been an academic question, but things changed if they were facing a demon seeking the key that would free him onto this plane, where he might range uninhibited.

Save for forge clerics and heroes.

Egon paused and studied the hill closer now. They were

still perhaps a mile from the nearest corner, traveling along what might have been the Emperor's main boulevard.

"May I examine the map?" he asked Anders, but the man was already close and holding it out.

Egon took a final look at fallen imperial glory and suppressed a sigh at the fact that evil never seemed to fade. Nor greed and ambition.

He knelt where Cletus might contribute, as well as his two taller comrades.

"Your thoughts, Master Cleric?" Cletus asked.

"Water," Egon replied absently. "In the mountains, my father's palace at Tozhug stands atop the artesian well that eventually forms the main river of the kingdom, with three impossible mountains at his back and the enormous valley that holds Lake Xomath below him, turning into a larger river on the far side where it connects the various valleys. There are creeks and such here, but a proper palace either needs either elaborate magic or mechanical connections to keep the cisterns filled. As you noted, Master Bard, forge magic."

Cletus beamed and stepped back with a courtly bow that left Egon snickering. Maybe he did serve a greater purpose here than meat shield.

He studied the map closer, noting the way streets had been laid in strange patterns that were too straight for cattle runs like back home, but not perfectly straight, either. A king might want tunnels that didn't pass under anyone else's palaces, to keep them from digging into his secrets themselves, so Egon focused on where water might flow.

This road went straight to the front gate, but there was one on his left that seemed to head directly towards the corner of the palace, except that it touched the wall just to one side of the tower. Keep the weight of the tower off the underground chambers where water could flow in from the river?

It felt like the sort of thing that had once been a road to the keep, perhaps when the city was much smaller. An underground river, perhaps? Covered over and forgotten in the last thousand years? He had heard of such things in other large cities, both in the distant east as well as the far south. Box it in with bricks and concrete and let it flow underground, while allowing you to erect buildings overhead with the land freed up.

A walled city held every square inch dear, after all.

Egon stood and studied the current terrain.

"You have something?" Anders asked.

Egon pointed to the map. Traced the line of the old street and how it emerged to the wall and the avenue below the walls and towers of the palace, headed roughly this way.

"We need to get to here, I think," Egon said.

Anders took the map and studied it now. He also looked up and nodded.

"Best if we double back a bit and traverse at the previous block, where we saw that one ruined tavern on the five-way corner," he announced.

Egon nodded. He had felt the call of the place. Someone had imbued it deeply with a warm hearth magic that still held traces all these centuries later. He wondered if an old bottle of whiskey or brandy might somehow survive this long without turning to vinegar.

Forge magic to seal it tight?

Egon made a note to ask his masters when he was next in the north, or to perhaps locate a brewer in someplace like Teregossa that might allow him to experiment.

The group organized and retraced their steps. Egon touched the wall of the tavern that had survived with his hammer as he went by, invoking a simple blessing for the memory of the publicans who had lived and died there, their love apparently powerful enough to stain the very stone with friendliness.

He turned and studied the sky now. Felt a chill wind that didn't even ripple the few weeds at his feet as it touched him.

"What is it?" Anders asked, looking all directions with his crossbow raised.

The others were equally nervous.

"We are close enough to a full moon?" he asked.

Cletus nodded.

"The afternoon grows late," Egon offered. "Not terribly late, but I doubt we will find a better place to rest for a time than this old tavern. Soon enough we will be underground, if my other guesses hold water, the darkness of night will not matter."

"Something watching us, my boy?" Cletus turned serious.

"Maybe," Egon agreed. "Or about to watch us, once the full moon rises."

"And this place?" Cletus pointed to the tavern wall that Egon still stood next to.

"Can't you smell the cookies about to come out of the oven?" Egon asked, half serious and half grinning.

Cletus and Ilvash both invoked and expressed their magic in different ways, but he could see their reaction as they opened their senses to the hearth within. The sudden smiles.

"Interesting," Ilvash spoke first. "How could this have survived?"

"I think that it would have been even stronger in the distant past," Cletus agreed. "Perhaps the point that anchored the entire neighborhood, both socially as well as magically. But I agree with our green friend. This is as good a spot as any for a bit of rest and some food. As with him, I suspect our friend, or his friends, will spy the first light of the full moon and use that to cast a beam of illumination into this city seeking us."

Egon led. Confined space, heavy armor, big hammer. The floor under his feet was covered over with several inches if dirt in places, but stone beneath that when he scuffed it with a heel. More than half of the roof overhead remained intact, though it had been wood.

Perhaps the magic of the hearth had protected it this long. Egon tried to visualize what the room might have looked like full, with a fire burning in the big stone hearth to warm the space and a tall Human man behind the bar tapping kegs and taking orders for food.

He moved forward warily, but the only thing that moved right now was a rat snake that looked up, spied him, and raced madly away for a hole in a side wall. Good. That meant that rodents would likely be scarce for now.

The others followed from some distance as he made his way to the enormous bar, again stone bricks rather than door, with a copper top that had been marred and rotted always to almost nothing. His own forge magic might not be enough to fix it, but Egon wondered if the hearth spirit could be roused from her slumber. It was obvious she had not entirely faded.

"What's through there?" Ilvhash asked.

Cletus was walking close behind Egon, with a thin blade in one hand. Ilvash walked right behind the man and he only came up to her chest, so she could see over him, even as short as she was.

"Kitchen," Egon guessed. "Maybe a cellar. Mind the floor beneath your feet. It turns to wood behind the bar where I'm standing, but seems to be holding up."

He was the heaviest, by far, so if it would hold him, the others would be safe, as long as they weren't close to him.

Egon moved to the doorway and studied things. Kitchen,

with a flat-top wood stove that had been made of something enchanted enough that it almost looked new even today. Piles of dust nearby that might have been wood, plus a rotted tin bucket holding coal at one time but empty now. Holes in the walls where shelves had once hung before falling, leaving broken glass and metal shards at his feet.

There. A trapdoor that went down to the cellar, covered over with wood. Egon approached and knelt down. As with the stove, the wood was in remarkable shape.

Closer up, it had been etched with a sharp knife and enchanted to the point that he half-expected it to glow. Preservation magic? His mother would know, were she here, but Egon rarely cooked, so much of the kitchen *esoterica* passed over his tall head.

"Cletus, could you examine this please?" Egon called. "Ilvash and Anders, too. I'll watch the front."

The walls around the kitchen were intact, and enough of a second floor had survived to protect all this from the elements. He moved his weight over the sill and let them kneel down to oohs and aahs as they touched that door.

"Intact, I think," Cletus pronounced. "Locked in some arcane manner, even yet today, but we ought to be able to unravel it enough to slip it open. Craftsmanship of this quality should never be broken, after all. It has held all this together for so long, 'twould be a most terrible shame to end it over something so unnecessary as sheltering us for a few hours."

Egon caught the Puck's wink and settled himself to keep anything from sneaking up on them. From inside the tavern, it was almost easy to touch his magic, so he extended a bit of Brese's love to the walls around him. Shore them up some, and let the old magic renew itself.

Ilvash did something now and he saw a faint glimmer seem to wrap everything from the old threshold inward in a splash of gold sparkles that faded quickly. He turned to ask what she had done but she smiled.

"This hearth spirit already wants to protect us from the cares of the outside world," she said. "Like you, I just added a bit of power to it, but I think it will also hide us from creatures that we expect to be hunting us tonight."

Egon nodded. A good tavern took your cares away. Let you hide from the weight of the outside world. Had they invoked such a thing by stepping in? He would have thought that all the power in the city would have corrupted it, but perhaps the old publicans had marked this land off and enchanted it special. It certainly had that feel to it. Nobody since had focused their enmity on the place, so it had stood like a watchtower, holding itself and this intersection well enough that it had spoken to each of them as they originally passed.

He placed the flat face of his hammer on the copper of the bar and let some more power flow through it. The tables and chairs in here had all rotted, but the stone held. Perhaps this building could be the anchor of something new, once he and his friends were able to clean some of the city out.

Or he came back with other friends later to complete that portion of the chore, after thwarting a mad Dwarf.

"Lad, your senses and your luck hold true," Anders called quietly.

Egon glanced back to see the trapdoor open, with light emerging from a cellar.

Light? After this long? Impressive magic indeed.

He made the sign of the Goddess in the air and pushed it outwards as a bane against all fell creatures, embracing the power of the hearth spirit and trying to call her up from her slumber. Something seemed to nod in his direction, so Egon hoped that she would shelter and protect them from what he knew was coming.

Then he moved to the kitchen as the other three slipped aside. First down into what he had been expecting as a dark hole, but the flow was the warm gold of torches.

He had a blink that jarred his very soul as he was suddenly back in the throne room.

"Egon?" Cletus asked.

"The light is the same here as my dream," he said. "Magical torches set to burn forever, but I thought that such things died when their wizard passed?"

He was looking at Ilvash, but she just shrugged, yet a journeyman enchanter in many ways.

"Perhaps the hearth spirit holds them dear," Cletus offered.

Egon grunted noncommittal and addressed himself to the stairs, shield and hammer ready for whatever might have remained hidden for so long.

Down eight feet, turn left on a landing. Egon paused there and looked over a space that had been hollowed out of the stone underneath the bar. Four more feet down and he was in a thing similar to his father's office, minus most of the books. There was a table and a chair, both still in good if scarred condition. A standing cabinet with drawers and a place to do sums and accounting.

But it was the far side of the space that drew his eye. Beyond a camp bed that still had sheets and a blanket were barrels, standing silently in the space like guards, from pins and firkins all the way up to butts and puncheons, each marked with a flavor and the master who brewed it.

And a wall held wine in glass bottles and even what looked like distilled liquors.

How had all this survived?

But the hearth spirit was stronger here when he opened his soul to her. She had held entropy at bay with the help of those enchantments on the trapdoor above him. Enough for beer and wine, perhaps.

"Indeed, Master Orc," Cletus said from the stairs. "Your instincts have led us true."

"Even idiot third sons like me occasionally have good ideas," Egon nodded.

Cletus turned a deadly serious look at him.

"You are many things, Egon the Bold," the Puck announced in a hard, serious voice. "A fool is not one of them. Best you not think of yourself that way, even in jest."

Egon blinked in surprise, then considered the man's words, as well as his own. Back home, many had thought him foolish to give up a pampered, easy life as a prince, even for something as complicated as a scholar. Few other than his mother had understood the call that had turned him serious.

Egon had just absorbed all the abusive language and turned it on himself, even when the bullies were long gone and had probably forgotten by now.

He needed to do better.

Egon moved deeper and found a space where a dumbwaiter could lift these heavy barrels upstairs to be tilted and tapped. And a spot where it looked like a well had been driven into the ground, with a pump.

He sniffed, and fresh cookies surrounded him with love.

"I think we might just close the door above us for a time and perhaps rest and eat here," Cletus continued. "I would not have believed such a place yet existed in the *darkwilds*, but this gives me hope."

Egon moved to the chair and the table. Someone had been doing their accounts here, right up to the end, but there were no bodies, so they had been above and perished. Or fled afterwards, locking everything tightly behind them.

Egon decided to believe that the family had managed to escape to someplace like Teregossa and started a new bar.

That left his heart and soul in a better place than imagining them dying in such a calamity.

"Sit, Master Orc," Cletus said, hopping agilely up onto the table itself and settling. "Anders and Ilvash can rest on the edge of the bed and we shall enjoy a solid repast."

"Are those bottles intact?" Ilvash asked.

Egon opened his senses to them again.

"Two have gone bad," he said. "One of the stouts had a leak and has gone dry. But yes, the others appear intact."

Anders smiled, but Egon could only imagine what such magical bottles might be worth to the right folk, let alone the contents of such a bottle.

He would indeed have a long conversation with someone about adding glassmakers to the guild of forge clerics, one of these days.

EIGHT

HUNTED

THEY ATE and drank some of their own water, leaving those other bottles alone by silent agreement. Everyone smiled for the first time in days.

Egon rose when he was done and considered the well in the corner. There were rivers close, but all contained in embankments assembled by engineers or wizards, so he pressed his senses into the ground itself, seeking the place where the well had gone.

The earth under the city here had none of the spoilage of the ruins and rubble above, which gave him hope. If they could just remove a few feet at the top, this place could live again.

Of course, that included all the things that lived here.

A sound that never made it to his ears caused him to look up sharply with a hiss that brought the other three to their feet, blades or enchantments ready.

"What is it, lad?" Anders asked quietly.

"Something just entered the tavern above us," Egon said in a deliberate voice, moving the table to retrieve his instruments of warfare. "What is the time?"

"Enough past sunset that someone might have summoned a thing or a pack to seek us," Cletus said. "But I doubt they will be able to force the door, as I made a point to seal it back up when we were below."

Egon nodded and went to stand in the spot best able to defend the room. Not at the bottom of the stairs, but on the landing, where nobody could easily get deep enough to jump sideways into the room without him being close enough to bash at them as they did.

He felt/heard the wood above him creak in a manner it had not when he had walked there. Was the thing that much heavier? It was in the kitchen now, seeking.

Egon could almost place the beast above him, so he wondered if the publican's magic was guiding him now.

Whatever it was did not seem to be intelligent, at least in the sense of understanding the trapdoor. Egon didn't hear a hand rattling it from above. At the same time, both he and Ilvash had imbued the place with their own power, so perhaps they had woken the hearth spirit sufficient that she was sheltering them yet?

"Ilvash, how realistic could you make one of your illusions?" Egon whispered to the woman.

"What are you asking?" she countered.

"There was a rat snake when I first entered," he said. "It fled me immediately. Could you place something similar above, and then have it race out the back door ahead of whatever it is above us, and then merely vanish?"

She blinked at him a few times, then nodded. Egon returned to his watch, listening with half an ear as she began chanting quietly. He'd seen her summon some creatures from the woods, as well as conjure spirits from other planes. A real mouse or rat right now might be perfect, but a fey trickster playing practical jokes on a wolf might be even better.

Something happened. Egon felt the floor above him

creak as the thing up there shifted its weight suddenly and scrabbled on wood floors for traction, receding towards the door where the kitchen could take deliveries.

Egon pushed a pulse of magic up, seeking to see the interior of the bar. He could smell wolf. The creature hadn't marked the territory with his urine, but his presence had left a sour taste in the air itself. At the same time, it had chased after whatever Ilvash had done and left.

For how long was unknown. However, its presence had let them know that someone was watching. He didn't dare open the trapdoor for a while. Nor send enough magic out to look around that a mad Dwarf might spy them and know the truth.

"I think it would be best if we assumed that our Dwarven friend has made allies," Cletus spoke. "Perhaps the night is more dangerous than we feared?"

"What about Jojo?" Egon asked.

Anders laughing was not the response he expected.

"She'll be fine," the man said. "Probably looking forward to stomping and goring anything that annoyed her. There was a reason I had you both wear smell wristlets when you first met her. Otherwise, she would not have been so friendly."

Egon could see that. Two tons of hair and horn. Even large wolves would be in trouble, trying to get inside with her, though she might be at risk later, when she decided she wanted some water.

Water. He had been thinking about the well.

Egon moved to the pump and worked it a few times. It had some rust, but that broke loose and he got water up into a basin. A quick blessing served to cleanse it, though he got the impression that it might not be necessary.

But something caught his attention as he stared at the wall in front of him.

"Master Cletus?" he said hesitantly.

"What is it?" the Puck asked, moving close.

Egon reached out a hand and tapped a spot where the bricks didn't seem to line up. A seam, except that there shouldn't be one there. If the building had settled, it would have done so differently.

"If I may?" Cletus asked, so Egon backed out of his way and watched the Puck cast something. "Indeed, Egon the Bold, you seem to live a charmed life. This is a false wall concealing a door."

"Can you open it?" he asked, already wondering what might need to be hidden even deeper than the magics above them.

"A moment," the Puck said.

Egon watched him move around a bit and touch a few places, almost absently.

"Ah, one is facing the well and pumping," Cletus said. "Master Egon, could you raise the handle but not lower it again?"

Egon did. Cletus touched a spot and the whole wall shifted backwards on hinges, revealing a tunnel beyond.

This one was much less ornate and well-kept. Spiderwebs gave evidence that life existed down here, but there were not tracks in the dust.

"Master Wilson, one of the torches, if you would?" Cletus asked.

Cletus went first, holding a flaming torch that might burn forever, using it to clear cobwebs and evict bugs. Egon walked immediately behind him, where the Puck might slip behind him in the blink of an eye if something jumped out.

"Catacombs?" Egon asked.

"I know not, my good man," Cletus replied, wielding the torch like one might a sword.

The tunnel was cramped for an Orc, though the average

Human could traverse it. He had to duck regularly so as to not bash his head on low beams or stones, and walk down the center of the five-foot-width to keep from brushing the sides. At least it ran straight.

They went about thirty feet and it came to another door. Barred from this side, so Cletus had him lift the bar and pull it inwards to reveal what was beyond.

Huh.

Not a catacombs, but an underground river. Interesting.

Egon wondered if the tavern had once been an inn at a crossroads outside of town, before Gillanish began its long rise to power and size that saw the place behind him engulfed into the city itself. A place like that on the road, perhaps at a ford, would be perfect for an enterprising brewer. Especially with as much trade and wealth as had flowed into the city over the millennia.

Marble stones had been laid down by a wizard at some point, forming a bed that felt ten or twelve feet deep, sloped too sharply to walk down, were you of a mind. The lateness of the season meant that it was much lower than spring floods might raise it, but there were walkways on either side, and Egon could see a bridge in the near distance by the light of Cletus's torch.

"Will it lead us to the palace?" someone asked. Might have been Ilvash, but Egon wasn't paying that close attention.

He had pushed his magical senses both directions to understand what this river was and how it had been created. Powerful magic. Several enchanters, because the stone itself had different flavors and hues as he watched it.

"Egon?"

He blinked.

"The palace?" Ilvash asked.

He turned to his right and looked. Orcish eyes could see

farther in darkness than just about anyone else, but the tunnel faded into darkness.

"It seems to be headed that direction," he hazarded a guess, orienting himself with the roads overhead.

If this was the right place, he had intended to look closer to that tower for something like a storm drain that might let them down here.

"I shall continue as your torchbearer then," Cletus announced with a laugh. "Master Egon shall follow, then Ilvash. Anders will cover us from the rear.

"What of the above?" Anders asked.

"Someone seeks us," Cletus turned serious. "It is my reasonable expectation that they will continue to do so until they find us, or we them, but I would greatly prefer if such a confrontation took place much later, that we might get into the palace and perhaps understand the nature of our quest in greater depth and detail."

Get close, kill things, as Egon translated it. He studied the water, but it had a brackish, ugly taint about it. As though it had been exposed to the surface enough to pick up some of the corruption and bring it below.

The well had gone deep into the clean earth.

They were in a darker realm now.

NINE
GOOSE

EGON COULD NOT HAD SAID what alerted him. The thing made no sound. Caused no ripple in the water.

One moment, nothing. The next, Egon had pivoted, stepped back and hip-checked Ilvash into the wall, away from the water, even as a long, toothy snout on a neck like a giant goose's had tried to latch onto her arm.

Enamel teeth made a hideous grinding sound as they clamped onto the edge of his shield and tried to pull him into the water instead.

Egon continued the turn that he had started and slammed the ballpeen head into the side of the creature's skull.

It squawked and reared up, hissing like a goose, but without any feathers on its plucked skin. Dark, beady eyes locked onto him and Egon snapped his shield out to distract the thing. It took the bait and tried to bite his shield again, exposing the skull to another strike.

Ilvash had recovered from her surprise and cast a spectral bolt of gold that missed, causing the water to foam madly instead. Anders fired his crossbow, and then reached for his sword.

Cletus, that rude little man, slipped under Egon's shield again and reached out with his torch, caressing the creature's neck with the open flames. It didn't like flames, as it reared back shrieking and turned to flee.

Egon put his back into the blow and something snapped like a wishbone where the head met the neck. More cries, but it flopped over and started to float now, the slow movement of the water more of a drift than anything.

"What was that?" Egon asked. "Felt like a demonic goose."

"You would not be entirely wrong," Anders spoke up.

The man reached out with his sword and speared the corpse, dragging it a little closer to the bank where he could grab the broken head with his hand. The beast turned around as the current carried it, but Anders planted his feet and held firm.

Plucked goose, maybe. The neck was as big around as his wrist. The beak had teeth from gripping and tearing flesh. The body had been moving underwater as it approached, but floated now, with fins rather than wings, so it was an aquatic form, rather than a aerial one.

"They used to be bigger, but time turned them from giant lizard forms into birds," Anders said. "Not all of them flew. Some, like this one, were sea monsters in their distant past. The magic has brought that part of them out again."

Egon watched him chop the neck quickly and then wrap the whole head in an oilskin cloth that went back into his bag.

"Main predator?" Egon asked.

"Most likely," Anders nodded. "There will be small things that fled from it, but few that were a threat to it, at least around here."

Egon fixed his shoulders and started to move again, but Ilvash caught his elbow.

"Thank you," she said in a serious tone.

He smiled. Egon hadn't been acting to save her like a hero in a fable, but moving automatically to kill something that was a threat. Still, both actions had the same outcome.

"Doing my job," he said with a sharp nod, turning and moving back up to the front again.

There would be other things out there he needed to face.

TEN

PALACE

THEY WERE CLOSER, perhaps had arrived. Egon felt the weight of the tower overhead, even though it was off to one side. The mass had caused the earth itself to feel heavier here. When he invoked a bit of magic, he could even see where the most recent set of palace walls were above them, running at an odd angle to the tunnel they were in.

Getting here, they had crossed the river via stone bridges several times, taking side corridors whenever the one they were in started to flare away from the path he was following in his head.

Ahead of them, an iron grate crossed the entire gap with holes small enough that only the Puck could make it through. Egon could probably bash his way through, but he saw no reason to announce where they were to anyone that might be close enough to hear them.

Or magical enough.

"Ah, we have arrived," Cletus announced. "Not that I was doubting you, my boy, but a few of those turns had me wondering if we'd perhaps been led astray. Glad to see I was wrong."

Egon just grinned at the little man. Both of them could admit to being wrong, which was always good. He hadn't been, but even Egon was willing to agree that he'd had the same opinion as the wee little Puck.

"Now, let us see to the way," Cletus continued. "Ilvash, if I could impose upon your arcane studies?"

Egon and Anders swapped ends now, with the Human ready to fire his crossbow at anything approaching from beyond the grate and Egon at the rear in case another something emerged from the black waters for a bite. The two in the middle moved quickly at whatever it was they did, and Egon heard a sharp ping of metal on metal, followed by the screech of hinges in need of grease.

A door was revealed from the way the grate had opened, and Egon moved into Cletus's shadow again.

"Perhaps, my dear friend, it would be best if you trailed me now by a bit," Cletus announced. "Having penetrated to the heart of the old conspiracies, I will be expecting a variety of traps and other silliness that might have survived all those centuries, much the way our dear tavern did the same."

"How far?" Egon asked simply.

"Give me twenty-five feet lead," Cletus decided. "Close enough that you can arrive quickly in a pinch, but not so close that your immense weight triggers anything that might have missed me before I could see it."

Egon nodded and waited. The grate went into the water, as well, so he presumed that the demonic goose lizard thing could not have come past there, but that also meant that something bigger inside might not have been able to escape ere now.

Egon considered the pathway now. If he was designing a trap, it might just be a slab that would dump someone into the water, demon-infested or not, and let them drown or be eaten. He didn't have a pole to test, but Egon guessed that the waters here were about six to seven feet deep. Enough that he could touch, and hop up to breathe, but he wasn't sure how well the others could swim.

Not everyone had an enormous lake in their front yard growing up, in whose freezing waters they were expected to swim and fish. But everyone knew how soft southerners were.

Almost immediately, Cletus held up a hand.

"Indeed, that was fast," he announced. "A few moments while I ascertain the nature of this mechanism and defeat it for you."

Egon watched beyond the Puck, but the tunnel just kept going out of sight and even the torch did not do much beyond twenty feet or so. He listened instead and heard only Cletus humming softly to himself as he worked.

"There, I believe that we have surmounted our current difficulties," Cletus said. "Egon, if you would step forward?"

He did. Nothing jumped out at him, or buckled under his feet. No monsters appeared.

"Excellent," Cletus said. "Anders, if you close the grate, it will lock, but Ilvash and I both have the word that will open it later."

Behind, a clanging as the grate protected their rear again.

Egon studied the walls. Better shape that even the river they had been following before. Not new, but not suffering from centuries of neglect. He wondered what magics had been used to smooth and polish everything, or keep time from damaging.

Forge magic, perhaps, or something like it, but on a scale he found truly impressive. As though dozens or hundreds of his kind had come together to do this work.

Two more grates presented themselves, as did half a dozen other traps that seemed more to keep the average vagabond out than a dedicated professional. Unless Cletus was much more than he seemed, which he gave flashes of occasionally.

Egon was a cleric with a hammer. You got what you saw with him and dealt with it.

Finally, they had come to a door. Wood, banded top and bottom with heavy iron riveted in. Orc-scale, at that, with ten foot of clearance and nearly five feet of width.

"I believe we have truly arrived," Cletus announced in a much more serious voice. "Behind us were the grounds, if you would. This door is the access point to the palace itself, and the tunnels and cellars underneath that artificial hill that was once a ziggurat above."

The group had assembled again, just outside that door.

"Do we pursue the vision Egon had?" Ilvash asked. "That throne room is near to the top of the place. Or do we follow the rumors and visions that suggest the depths?"

"The map was made by folks that almost got to the throne room itself before retreating," Anders said, drawing their attention to the thing. "They did not make it in before they fled, whoever they were, so as far as we know, nobody has seen those grounds in centuries. I would not put much faith in them."

"Agreed," Cletus said. "Additionally, I would remind you that we are at depth now, so it might be easier to simply try to remain down here and seek our goal. We can always work our way to the heights, but the tunnels, if nothing else, will greatly limit the size of any beast that might wish to do us harm here."

Egon grunted his agreement. He'd be on point, ready to bash and block. Maybe summon some of Brese's power should the dead have risen to the call of another necromancer.

Whatever had summoned Arinwa Hollenc and Vorlothe the Dwarf had to be dark and evil, just based on stories and personal experience. Egon could see some foul demon, with perhaps a toehold in this plane of existence, working to adjust things.

There had been several armies of dead from which one might cause skeletons and other creatures to rise again. But hammers did a perfectly serviceable job of ending skeletons, in a manner that swords and crossbows could not.

"I shall open this door quietly but step back, lest something on the other side rouse," Cletus continued. "Egon shall hold the front, while the rest of us remain a bit back in the hallway, ready to provide him assistance. Ilvash, I might remind you that undead are generally immune to the sorts of illusions that can frustrate the living. It might be time for you to bring out the heavy magics, as it were."

"Indeed," she agreed.

Egon had no idea what that might entail, other than Cletus had sought her out specifically. He nodded now as the Puck unlocked the door and did something that caused it to open without laying a hand on it.

It was good that the Puck withdrew immediately, though. Through the doorway, Egon saw men rising from bunks and drawing swords, each moving in an eerie silence.

He looked closer and saw that they were all skeletons, dressed in the gray and blue uniforms and armor from his dream, skinless faces and clacking jaws as they perhaps tried to warn him or taunt him.

Egon smiled and held up his hammer before him. It had already begun to glow ever so slightly.

"By the power of Brese, I command you to be *undone*!" he yelled. "Return to your rest and bother the living no more!"

A flash of light filled the room. It was a barracks on closer look, which made sense. You would want soldiers guarding a place like this where a thief might sneak past all the magical and mechanical contrivances.

Much harder to get by a dozen men with swords.

More than half of them faltered now as Brese lit the room with her glory. Necromancy was not quite the emotional and magical antithesis of forge magic, but it was close enough. His kind made things and unmade them. Skeletons represented a false life at odds with all things natural.

Eight of them sundered to dust as he watched, leaving four clacking forward, swords in hand. Not one held a shield of any kind, and the armor on their bodies shows centuries of rust and decay.

Egon stepped into the first one, even as it raised its sword, and bashed it in the head with his hammer. Again, Brese blessed him and a flash of light erupted from the blow, rendering the skeleton a puddle of bony fragments on the floor.

Two more came at him, but Egon held the doorway and they could not flank him. One struck his shield. The other hit the frame and his sword broke off midway.

Before Egon could reply, Ilvash stepped up and blasted one in the face with a bolt of energy that rippled with a rainbow of colors. It immediately turned and hacked at the skeleton behind it, even as that one tried to get to Egon.

Egon crushed the chest of the one with the broken sword and then just stood there defensively as the other two hacked each other to bits.

"What was that?" he asked when they were finally done.

"I lack the power to raise the undead," Ilvash replied with a tight grin. "But I know enough to control them for a short period of time. These were under the domination of someone, or rather, its orders from the way they reacted."

"Does the thing know we have arrived?" Egon asked.

"I don't think so," she shrugged. "This sort of magic is created one and then left in place. I doubt they would have messengers running about and checking in, expecting that a room full of undead warriors would normally be sufficient."

"And indeed it would be, in most instances," Cletus chuckled. "Unless one of course took the time to recruit a priest with a deep and abiding hatred of such creatures and the power of his Goddess to do something about it. Then the outcomes might end up entirely different from what one might have planned."

Egon nodded. Cletus had a plan, and had found specific skill sets and abilities to help him implement it. An young enchanter who was the daughter of two powerful wizards. A tallowmaster who was intimately familiar with the *darkwilds*.

And an idiot third son prince who had found a different calling as a warrior. Except he wasn't an idiot, and he needed to remember that. People were counting on him to be their shelter from the storm.

A hero.

Egon stepped into the room and looked around.

"Would there be anything of value to be recovered?" he asked.

Gold and silver could wait for their return, but he didn't expect there to be such as was worth the time to go through everything.

Cletus stopped in the middle of the room and slowly rotated in place, so Egon assumed he was using his own magical senses.

"Nothing," he said. "Not unexpected. Let us press our case onwards."

A door on the far side of the room connected to a hallway. This room had been large enough for a dozen men to live in reasonably close quarters with beds on two walls, a jakes through a door, and a spot to cook. Guardroom.

Beyond, they found several rooms of storage and what Egon took to be officer's quarters. Nothing of any value remained sufficient to cause them to search. Egon supposed that a captain might have acquired a bit of magic in his or her time, but if so, it had probably been with them when they died on the wall or in the street fighting.

Just rotted barrels and trunks, piled up and then fallen over as time ate away at their strength. The tavern stood larger and larger in his mind, for having withstood everything to date. He would start there and build a new city, one of these days, perhaps.

"Ilvash, what can you see?" Cletus asked as they paused at one of their regular stops to listen.

Egon watched her close her eyes and stand perfectly still for a time.

"We are below something," she murmured. "Only a level or so, but I can sense something on the edge of wakefulness."

"Can you tell what?" Cletus pressed.

"No," she shook her head, eyes still closed and doing something they never taught a poor priest. "I don't see a thing, so much as gather impressions in a darkened room. Several things sleep restlessly, if that makes any sense."

"Indeed it may," Cletus said. "We are not too late, but time still flies and we should move."

Egon took the lead now, moving with Cletus close beside him and stopping him from time to time to inspect things, but they were inside the palace now, and did not expect traps.

Watchers would be more likely.

Stairs. A broad, stone staircase leading up. Not as elegant as an emperor might demand, but well-made. Egon knelt and noted the marks of masons who had cut and polished them, rather than relying on the power of wizardry to do the job.

There was dust on them, from the stillness of the air, but he could see no tracks that had disturbed things in a long time.

"The next level up would be roughly equivalent to the old ground floor of the place before it was raised?" he asked.

"It would," Cletus nodded, "but has not seen the light of day in perhaps two millennia at this point.."

He still had his torch, lighting the way for the others, but Egon could see beyond it to where the stairs ended at a landing above. Or the next floor upwards.

"Wait here a moment," Egon said to Cletus, nodding to the light.

The Puck nodded and the others slipped to one side.

Egon took the first step slowly, turned a little sideways so that his shield was directly in front and he could sidestep up without having to take his eyes off the darkness to count each step.

He paused, just below the top, where only his eyes were high enough to see.

Another chamber, empty but this one was filled with rubble suggesting that a mob had rampaged through at some point, spilling everything.

He smelled something on the air. Something rank and bitter.

Wolf. One of those bastards had marked this room, and done it recently enough that it might still be damp.

Egon saw a doorway down a bit. The door had been torn from the top hinge and hung drunkenly against the wall. Beyond it, he saw movement.

Anders had been right. Those things were huge. Small horses. Two of them were standing in a hallway with their tails this way. Hopefully, there was no breeze that would carry his scent to them.

Egon turned to glance down the stairs and saw Cletus

watching. Putting his finger to his mouth for silence, he gestured the Puck to join him. Anders had the torch at this point, but they needed darkness around them.

Cletus joined him and stood on a step with a view.

"Oh, indeed," he murmured, leaning close to murmur in Egon's ear. "Our old friend the Dwarf has recruited some rather frightful assistants. We need to get around them, as combat will make too much noise at present."

"They will smell us coming," Egon pointed out.

"Perhaps not, my gigantic friend," Cletus grinned. "You keep watch for a moment."

And the Puck vanished back down the stairs. Egon wasn't sure if the two Humans could see in this darkness. The sun should have set a while ago, so it would be the middle of the night, as well as being underground.

There was no more light than a good candle in that chamber where the two wolves were. Enough for him and Cletus, at least.

The other three joined him after a few minute, minus the torch, so it must be hanging down in that hallway somewhere.

"Anders will add some oil to your armor and flesh," Cletus whispered. "It will eliminate all scent for a time, and Ilvash and I will do some magic to hopefully hide us as we pass."

Egon nodded. Of course a tallowmaster would know how to eliminate smells. You needed to be able to sneak up on things to hunt them. He remained still while Anders wet a rag from a vial and rubbed the liquid over him.

"We're good," the man whispered a moment later.

"Excellent," Cletus said. "Everyone grab hands. Egon, if you could keep your shield handy but hang your hammer, Ilvash shall turn us all invisible and I will cast something that will silence the tread of Orcish boots on stone floors."

Egon grinned. The others all moved with great silence, but he was in heavy armor. It made noise.

Ilvash took his hand in hers now and did something quietly with her other and everyone was just gone.

Yes, indeed a most wonderful way to move about. He felt the woman tug on his hand now and he let her lead him up the steps and into the ruined room that awaited.

The two wolves seemed restless as they went by, but did nothing more than sniff uncertainly at the air and paw a bit at the stone floor. It was as if something wasn't right, and they weren't intelligent enough to seek out an answer.

Ilvash tugged him gently along in perfect silence, past the wolves and through a far doorway that looked important. They stopped there and the door behind him swung shut suddenly, the bolt sliding into place firmly.

At once, the spells vanished and Cletus and Anders smiled from the door.

"That should keep those two at bay for a time," Cletus said. "Remind me that we may need to deal with them later, but I would prefer they be stuck over there for now."

Egon heard the wolves scratching now at the far side of the door. However, it had been made for sieges, not oversized demon dogs and it would hold.

They were in another hallway that felt familiar to Egon.

"This is like the antechamber to one of my father's grand rooms for sitting in judgment, back home," he said. "Not the big throne room, but the one where everyone gathered for royal power to be dispensed in public."

"I see," Cletus nodded. "Perhaps we should be prepared for what lies beyond, then. This might be our destination, and it appears that we are late to the party."

Egon drew his hammer and adjusted his shield. He moved to the far end of the chamber and listened.

Chanting. Never a good sign, especially not in a supposedly-abandoned and probably-haunted palace.

The others joined him at the door and peeked into the room.

Lights. Not as many as that throne room had had above them, but enough to fill the space. It felt like a small cathedral, with vaulted ceiling overhead and two rows of pillars dividing the room into thirds down the long axis.

Four more of the wolves were all focused inward, watching as a group of Humanoids on a slight dais were making noise. Sounded like an incantation of some sort.

The wall beyond them was marked off with a variety of strange carvings that resolved as portraits as Egon studied them.

This, then, was the imperial crypt. Each of those spots along the front wall held the body of an emperor. The group had broken into one and pulled out the sarcophagus from within. The top lay off to one side and they were performing some incantation over it now.

"Egon, they must not succeed at opening it," Cletus said fervently. "Ilvash, kill the wolves to clear him a path forward. Egon, we will be right behind you."

He had no idea what might happen when they completed whatever task they were after. Based on his dream, he suspected that the body of Arinwa Hollenc lay within, hidden there by his demonic master in the aftermath of the man's original failure.

Egon began to jog forward, not sure what the situation needed, but certain that Cletus was right. He needed to be closer.

Ilvash, in addition to her mastery of illusion, apparently also studied many other forms of arcane lore and power. A ball of red light flashed past him as he moved and exploded in the midst of the wolves, erupting into a column of fire reaching nearly to the vast ceiling in here.

The smell of singed dog assailed his nostrils. T the spell had been successful, as all four were blackened corpses.

Ahead of him, the chanting ceased. The group on the platform looked around and then at him in utter surprise before they began to reach for weapons. All except the Dwarf in the middle. He continued to chant and started to reach into the stone coffin for something.

Egon did the only thing he could think of.

"Brese, guide me now!" he yelled, invoking her power and hoping that she would listen to a fool of a prince, especially one trying to become a hero.

He was already running, so Egon reared back and threw his hammer overhand across the space.

Vorlothe, intent on whatever evil prize had drawn him thus, never saw it coming. The hammer struck him square in the chest and bowled him over backwards in a flash of light so intense that Egon wondered if he might have gone blind.

There were a half dozen of them up there: Elf, Human, and another Orc he didn't recognize.

Egon charged.

ELEVEN
VORLOTHE

EGON WAS UNARMED, facing half a dozen foes, and had interrupted them in the middle of some terrible arcane ritual. Behind him, Cletus, Ilvash, and Anders, but they were none of them warriors, and the six in front of him were.

He had to take them all out before they could react.

At the last minute, Egon invoked that bit of magic that had made him twelve feet tall to fight the lizard, and then just dove headlong into the group, arms spread wide and carrying them all with him into a pile atop the already-woozy Dwarf.

Egon recovered first and jumped to his feet, even as the others laid there moaning.

Except that the Dwarf had recovered as well. And gotten to his feet with that stupid, glowing ax in hand, while Egon's hammer was over there somewhere under the bodies.

"You DARE?" Vorlothe snarled, stepping right onto the chest of the Orc and casting something ugly and loud.

Egon just barely managed to get his shield in the way. The bolt still hit hard enough that he felt steel bend, one of the rivets popping right out and falling away like a diamond from the sky. He stumbled backwards over someone's foot and felt his butt slam into the side of the sarcophagus.

Help had almost arrived, but Egon watched a magical bolt bounce off of some shield that Vorlothe had raised, splashing instead.

"DIE!" Vorlothe screamed.

Egon's shield stopped that ax a second time, but he could tell from the sound that it made that a third blow would take it and his arm off, so he tossed it in the Dwarf's face instead and looked around for a weapon.

Something.

Anything.

The Dwarf's allies were starting to get themselves organized as well. He had no time, and his friends hopefully weren't crazy enough to bums rush a mob of warriors.

His eyes fell onto the interior of the sarcophagus, spied the Elf warrior inside, laid out for a proper burial with a sword across his chest.

Egon knew it was a stupid idea, but he'd run out of other solutions.

He grabbed the blade.

And immediately understood what a terrible mistake he'd made.

The Elf was Arinwa Hollenc. The blade was *Ediade*. Soultaker.

It awoke in his hands.

Everything was suddenly tinged red in Egon's eyes, like a fine mist of arterial blood had been spritzed from an atomizer.

He could taste the Dwarf's fury as it gave way to sudden fear.

"NO!" Vorlothe screamed, hacking overhead with his own glowing blade.

Ediade intercepted the blow on its own and knocked the ax to one side, almost negligently.

Then it lashed out and drank the blood of the Human on the right, only now on his knees and looking around for a sword he would never find.

The blood in the air grew stronger, almost orgasmic in smell.

Egon slashed at the Orc now and chopped him in two with a single blow as Vorlothe backpedaled away.

More blood. More power.

Ediade was on the verge of waking fulling.

A tiny voice in the back of Egon's soul knew that he would never recover if it did. Never be anything but the servant of the blade and its own master.

He would become Arinwa Hollenc reborn, but now he knew that the Champion of Darkness had just been a hollow shell driven forward by a demon given flesh in the form of a sword.

Still he felt his eyes glow red enough to light the darkness.

Another blow and an Elf died screaming at his feet.

Vorlothe threw a magical bolt at him now, but *Ediade* laughed with Egon's mouth and deflected it, just as Vorlothe had.

The Dwarf ran. Abandoned his allies to the slaughter, to which Egon and *Ediade* were only so happy to fulfill.

He stood amidst a pile of bodies, twelve feet tall and filled with the gore and passion of undeath itself.

"Egon, you must fight it," a voice intruded.

He looked down at the tiny fool who had thought to thwart him.

No, little man, he rumbled. ***We have become. Let all the world fear us now***.

But that tiny voice recognized the Puck that had first

approached him the same day as the fool Vorlothe had sought to deflect them from the quest. That-which-was-Egon cried out inside for them to hold. That these were friends.

But *Ediade* recognized no friends. Only victims.

He took a step forward and slammed into a wall of force that someone had erected across his path. Egon reached out but it was solid. And higher than he could reach.

"Egon, resist it," the fool Puck called. "You are stronger than evil."

Ediade tapped the wall with the sword and heard it ring like a bell.

He reached deep and swung with his immense stature and strength. Felt the blow rattle the wall. It did not shatter, but a second blow would do.

He smiled at the three mortals below him.

"We must flee for now," the Puck ordered the others. "Perhaps the worst has come to past."

Worst? No little man. The greatest thing ever. I have power, and nothing in this world is prepared to stop me.

Ediade watched the three flee, even as his second blow shattered their pitiful wall into eldritch fragments that tinkled on the stone like broken glass.

He laughed and strode forward after them, his mighty legs making short work of the distance.

Except that the fools who built this place thought too small. The doors and hallways were for Humans. He would have to advance and his knees to go after them now.

Ediade reached within himself somewhere and found the font of power that sustained him, recognizing that other creature he was inhabiting. They fought for control, but the Orc was willing to release that thing that kept them gigantic.

With a thought, they shrank back down to normal size, still a terrible seven feet tall, but the others had made good their escape in the confusion.

Ediade looked back at the room where his old body had been placed to wait. His mount. Corpses lay strewn, and that Dwarf had fled through a different door, but he would make a useful servant at some point.

Or the latest victim. Whichever.

The blade glowed with enough light to see, even here in the dimness of the lower palace. He got to the door and found that they had somehow locked and barred it from this side, so *Ediade* lifted the beam and cast it noisily to one side. Beyond, he could hear noises, so he opened the door and confronted a pair of darkwolves.

The first snapped at him, so *Ediade* killed it, drinking its blood and whatever pitiful bits of soul such a creature might have. Hardly more than the Dwarf's minions had possessed.

The second darkwolf closed, locking it's jaws onto the steel-cased arm where he would have held his shield, had that Harridan not broken it. That just anchored it for a killing blow.

Pathetic.

Had creatures of the modern age turned into such weak things?

Except that he rode a powerful warrior now. Orc, which he had never used as a mount before. Strong-willed and fighting him even now for possession of their body.

Ah, a priest of some hearth goddess from the north. How quaint. He would make a useful servant, as *Ediade* conquered the world again.

Around him, he recognized the fallen palace of the Gillanish Emperors. How long had passed, for it to be thus?

Ediade let the light of his blade guide him to a barely-remembered flight of stairs up. For a moment, he thought he heard a sound, but when he turned, there was nothing there.

Yes, the Puck and the two Humans. He had already forgotten about them in the blood-lust of killing. They would be hiding from him now, seeking a way out of this place before he could hunt them down.

The woman had been attractive, for a Human. Perhaps he would keep her as a plaything when he slaughtered the other two.

Ediade needed to touch the power of the darkness above. To revel in the passing of time that had rendered this world so passive that they had ignored him for however long.

He needed to fully awaken.

Then he could bring his evil back to an unsuspecting world.

TWELVE

THRONE ROOM

EDIADE LOOKED over the throne room as he stood quietly on a balcony and stared angrily at the beast below. In his memory, the room had been beautiful and elegant, lit with torches long since decayed and polished by an army of servants on a daily basis.

The roof had fallen in across nearly a third, crashing to the floor and leaving a layer of rubble that had been softened with age and dirty into something perhaps one might call a nest.

For a *thing*.

Ediade wasn't sure what to call it. It had not yet detected him, so the thing's sense of smell must be terrible, but he suspected that the eyes would be sharp.

It reeked of dark power, but not the kind that *Ediade* or his cousins might have created.

In form, it had elements of a bear and an owl. Long legs ending in talons. Arms with claws on the ends. Wings emerging from the back. Owl's face.

He guessed it at nine feet tall, and perhaps four hundred pounds. Equal to an Orc in plate, then, save that it could fly. The glowing blue eyes that occasionally looked up suggested mad intelligence or magical abilities as yet unknown.

What had happened here?

How had Gillanish fallen into such terrible straights that magical monsters slept where an emperor had once sat, and where an Elf named Arinwa Hollenc had once stood proudly?

Inwardly, he turned to the Orc. Unlike the Elf, this creature still fought him, but lacked an understanding of how to win.

Ediade was a demon. He only looked like a sword because that had been the form chosen for him by the mad wizard who had thought to conquer the world so many centuries ago.

"What happened here?" he demanded inwardly of the Orc.

"You failed," the priest replied through angry, gritted teeth. "Your war destroyed Gillanish, and for six centuries the place has been nothing but a blasted wasteland, populated by things like that beast below. Nobody even lives on this side of the river."

Ediade growled. Without an army, he could do nothing. From the Orc, he caught a name.

Teregossa. A poor kingdom to the west, outside of the old lands Gillanish had claimed. Something of a descendant of Karnegriand.

Ediade hissed as the memory returned. Crown Prince Mahyrst of Karnegriand. Killing him, even as he and Arinwa killed the Human.

So close, and then undone by a fool willing to sacrifice his immortal soul.

And he had succeeded. Six centuries?

Karnegriand no longer existed. Most of the old lands

were rearranged or abandoned, as he forced more and more information out of the Orc.

Stubborn, that one. Not stubborn enough, though.

"It would have been better had you let the Dwarf claim me," *Ediade* taunted the priest. "Then you might have been able to kill him and somehow defeat me again. Now, I have all your power, as well as my own. Nothing will stand before us."

The Orc boy grunted and fought. Gritted his teeth and tried to close his mind.

Ediade just laughed.

Below, a creature looked up. Spotted him on the balcony. Leapt into the air.

Ediade had forgotten the beast.

Now, it looked like he would have to slay it.

So be it.

The thing alighted on the rail and clamped down with razor-sharp talons, screeching in fury and hunger. *Ediade* thrust at it with the blade but the beast sidestepped and pecked, scarring the steel on his shoulder with the thing's beak.

Something glowing in those eyes reached into their combined mind and *Ediade* stumbled backwards a step before he caught himself.

Owl. Night terror for small rodents. The cry that froze them for the striking.

He lurched back another step as that terrible beak came for his arm, just managing to deflect it with the flat of the sword as he stumbled back another step.

It hopped off the rail and waddled towards him now, calling as though others might come to feast.

Ediade struck with the blade, feeling it cut feathers that felt like steel scales, but sufficient to draw some blood and a cry of rage and pain.

So, it could be killed.

Inside, the Orc fought him.

"Cease your struggles or you will get us killed!" he howled at the thing whose mind he shared.

"Good," the priest called back. "Let us die here and make the world that much better of a place."

Ediade was stunned, even as the stupid bird tried to grab him with its hands now. To draw him close like the bear might, and then maul him.

Arinwa had been a willing servant. A Champion of Darkness striding the world. This fool of a priest wanted to thwart him.

He slashed at the bird thing again, scoring an arm that wanted blood. It growled and flinched. *Ediade* struck it again.

This would be like chopping a tree down with a sword, a painfully-slow process that would take all day. And the tree was actively trying to kill him.

Ediade gave ground slowly, step by step, hacking and slashing any time a limb got close or threatened.

The beast fought on, maddened by pain or hunger now.

Or perhaps pure rage. If it claimed the throne room, perhaps it was the apex predator of the old city. He had seen in the Orc's memory where the city was nothing but ruins, a field of fallen and poisoned stone that would never grow crops sufficient for anything but monsters such as these.

Would he have to actually save the world before he could rule it? What a profoundly disgusting notion, but apparently his cousins had made this land too much like the planes of hell that they called home.

The bird snapped at him and *Ediade* ducked behind the doorway, then lunged forward and caught it in the keel with his blade. Yes, a telling blow.

It shrieked in shock and pain and hopped away from him, turning to flee and presenting a rear flank undefended.

Ediade struck in that moment and caught the beast square. It leapt as though to fly, but then collapsed across the rail with a fading wail of rage that ended with the beast falling forward off the balcony to slam into the ground below with a wet sound.

Ediade stepped up and looked around, checking the sky to make sure that the battle had not drawn others of the kind.

If the magic that created it had somehow managed to create more. Or worse, that such a thing bred true.

He had meant to conquer the world, not destroy it. What good was it to rule over shattered wastelands? He could return to the plane of his birth and do ***that***.

No, he need warm, pleasant lands. People. Victims that he could dominate.

The Orc had visions of a terrible north, cold and brutal where water froze for months at a time and fell from the sky as ice.

No, he would need places like Teregossa or Karnegriand. The warm southern lands. Perhaps he would head even farther away, and find places where the heat was like home, but that had never heard of Gillanish, nor *Ediade*.

Yes. That would to.

A sound snapped his head around. *Ediade* caught movement by the door where he had just fought. He lunged in that direction, intent on killing whatever it was.

Something barred his way, at least temporarily. *Ediade* jolted off of something unseen and stumbled, catching himself, even as the Human woman appeared at his feet.

Ah. Wizard. Yes. Illusionist. She had been invisible and stalking him.

Ediade smiled.

There would be other playthings later, after he had regained his power and slain all that knew the truth about him and his rebirth.

He could see the abject terror in her eyes, prone beneath him as he raised his sword up for a killing blow. The others had been little more than wild animals, even the ones on two feet. But this was a sorcerer. He would gladly consume her soul and use it to power all manner of power.

no...

Something held his hand. *Ediade* could not strike to kill her. He growled and heaved, but his muscles would not respond.

No.

Ediade struggled, turning this way and that, but the blade would not move. Muscles stood out as cords under his skin, but nothing he did could take a step, nor swing that killing blade.

And she was right there. Virginal, even. *Ediade* could taste that about her power, even as the blade turned a hard, brilliant crimson, aching for her blood.

NO!

The Orc. That was it. Fool priest was fighting him for control of the body. Was holding him somehow back from his first true meal in centuries.

"Release me!" *Ediade* screamed inside his head at the other one. The fool.

No, the Orc replied, holding them perfectly still, even as the woman finally found herself and began to scupper backwards from where she had fallen at his feet.

"Egon, catch," a voice intruded.

Ediade looked up and the Human male was there as well. He tossed something this direction, rather than casting it as a weapon.

The Orc's hammer, etched with his foolish hearth mistress on both sides of the head.

And yet it seemed perfectly normal to switch the blade from his right hand, where it threatened the girl, to his left. Almost automatic, as he reached out his hand and caught the hammer out of the air and gripped it.

And immediately understood what a terrible mistake he'd made.

The Orc roused now, having been almost in a slumber before. Sleep walking while *Ediade* controlled their body. The priest screamed inside his mind even worse than the owl had.

Ediade struggled, but the priest tapped wells of power and fury that his sleeping mind had forgotten about.

And then something opened his left hand, and the sword tumbled to the ground.

Ediade and the Orc fell beside it a moment later.

THIRTEEN

WAKEFUL

EGON HAD LEARNED at a young age to either water his wine, or drink something like juice or milk when the others decided to go in for a heavy bout of drinking. He'd never had a really bad hangover as a result.

Until today.

The sky overhead was made of stone. Well-worked, with mosaics pressed in by skilled artisans. The stone under his ass was cold. His hands were bound.

His head hurt.

Egon opened his eyes and squinted when the terrible torchlight wanted to send spears of pain through the back of his skull.

"How are you, my boy?" a far-too-damned-chipper-this-morning asked.

Egon closed one eye and cracked the other enough to see Cletus smiling down at him.

"Ow," he replied.

"Indeedly so, my young and foolish Orc friend," the Puck grinned. "That was truly a moment worthy of an epic, though I might have to edit it some in the retelling."

"As long as I look like less of a moron?" Egon asked.

"Hard to make you look worse, I think," Cletus nodded. "Is he gone?"

Is who gone?

But Egon understood the nature of the question. There'd been two of them in his head for the last however long. Talking. Ranting. Arguing. Fighting.

Hangover.

Bad one.

He closed his eyes and rooted around, finding dark spots like finger print smudges on his mother's fine crystal, but nobody besides himself.

"I think so," Egon said, feeling a pulse of magic echo his words much louder than he'd intended.

A hand moving caught his attention. Ilvash. Casting something.

Truth-sensing, most likely.

Her right eye was bruising nicely where he'd apparently elbowed her at some point.

The demon had, but it had been Egon's body.

"Sorry about that," he said to her.

She smiled weakly down at him.

"Thought you were about to eat me," she said in a forced camaraderie.

"He wanted to," Egon said. "That gave me a handle to finally fight him. Up until that point he'd been completely in control of our body. Seeing you did something and I was able to grapple him with my mind."

"As we suspected, thought not the manner in which I had originally intended to investigate, as it were," Cletus spoke up now. "Still, Anders understood my meaning in giving you the hammer. Brese seemed pleased with the result, to have broken you free from the thing's control."

"Ow," Egon repeated. "Feels like all three of you have

been beating me with sticks for the last hour. How soon until you'll be ready to untie me?"

Cletus looked at Ilvash and got a nod, so he reached down and the knots vanished in a puff of magical smoke.

"You're back now, my boy, and in control," Cletus said. "We might have done a few things to you while you were delirious and insensate, but they were for your own good."

Egon levered himself to a sitting position and then managed to not fall over when the whole world went woozy around him. He blinked too many times and eventually the horizon stopped meandering.

One hand went to Brese's symbol on his chest and he reached inside for her blessing. Much of her power had either been withdrawn, or used up fighting a demon, but he found enough now to grind off some of the pain from his bruises as a soft, white glow enveloped his body.

"Regardless of whatever, I will need a long nap soon," Egon said quietly. "Is there a safe place we can rest? Vorlothe is still around here somewhere."

"Indeed he is," Cletus nodded. "Given our options, we thought it better to pursue you and ignore him, rather than splitting up and risking both."

"How did you escape him? Me? Whatever?" Egon asked.

"While you were distracted with things, we merely used Ilvash's illusions to hide," Cletus laughed. "It seemed useful to let the two of you encounter those wolves and handle them for us."

Egon shifted now until he was kneeling, still a little unwilling to trust standing until he had some time to recover.

Ediade, the blade, lay nearby, pulsing under a piece of cloth that kept the light hidden.

Egon could still sense exactly where the blade and the demon were, even with his eyes closed.

"What do we do about that?" he asked, not making any motion towards it except to nod in that direction.

They would be concerned that the demon was about to grab him again.

Hell, he was nervous.

"For a time, Ilvash or I can loft it with the same sorts of magic that we've done before," Cletus said. "It would be best for all concerned if we kept it away from our friend as we made our departure. While there was talk of treasure to be had, I think that it would be best for everyone concerned if the blade took precedence at the moment."

Egon nodded.

"How do we destroy it?" he asked.

"That, good sir, is a task to which I had high hopes might be in the purview of a forge cleric." Cletus grinned, but Egon could see how forced it was.

He reached out and grabbed his hammer now, pulling it close and letting the weight of it ground him.

"Ask me tomorrow," he offered.

"Indeed I shall hold you to that, master Orc," Cletus nodded. "For now, I think it would be most useful for us to backtrack ourselves to the tavern, there to hide and thence to plan our moves that will allow us to evade the Harridan and whatever power or puissance he might be able to recruit, having lost all of his assistants to the kiss of a demon lover."

Egon struggled to his feet, eventually relying on Anders to hold him. The man held out Egon's shield, battered and not quite broken.

"It can be fixed," Anders said. "I have some of the tools back at the cart with Jojo."

Egon shrugged and strapped it to the outside of his backpack for now. Trying to use it in combat would be almost worse than not having it.

He paused, turning to walk over to where the owl

creature had fallen, already dead, lying now below in a pool of green ichor that had nothing to do with blood.

"You spy something?" Cletus asked jauntily from his knee. "Or remember?"

"Throne room," Egon said. He pointed. "The Captain was there when we entered. Arinwa fought him there and both died."

"As your memories would suggest, yes," Cletus prompted him.

"The blade and the wielder were hidden away by someone," Egon continued. "Placed in a sarcophagus where the Emperors of Gillanish normally resided, so perhaps one had been prepared for the man who died here that day. I have no memories beyond those deaths, but we know that nobody escaped from this room."

"What would that suggest, master cleric?" Anders was there on his other side.

Egon turned to Ilvash, now starting to look like a half-raccoon.

"After I sleep, I'll fix your eye," he offered apologetically. "Sorry again. "

She grinned.

"Do you have the strength left to look under the ground there?" he asked.

"Not from here," Ilvash replied. "What did you expect to see?"

"This sword was claimed," he said, pointing back to where *Ediade* lay. "What about the other one? The one the Captain killed Hollenc with?"

"Oh."

Egon nodded.

"It might still be there, somewhere."

FOURTEEN
RUBBLE

EGON WASN'T sure that it couldn't have waited, but Cletus had been insistent, so they found themselves back down a level from the gallery, walking around the place where that final, apocalyptic battle had been fought. He almost felt like two people watching the scene, separated by centuries.

Possibly three, since he also had memories of killing Mahyrst of Karnegriand on this ground.

The blade *Ediade* had been wrapped in a blanket and tied to Egon's pack, slung behind him now where he couldn't get at it without a lot of work.

He would be lying if he said he didn't hear it whispering to him.

But something else whispered as well, and that second voice provided him a calm salve.

There.

Egon stopped walking and turned to his right. The others were back a bit, watching him work with his ancient past, however strangely it had come about. He took four steps forward and looked down.

Touching a spot in the dirt before him, he looked the length of the great hall and realized that he was almost exactly down the centerline.

It had happened right here.

"Ilvash, this was the place," he said, scuffing the dirt with his heel and then walking over to stand next to Cletus.

She and Anders strode to the center now and looked around. The woman cast an incantation into the air and looked down. Egon watched her shift a little to her left and stop.

"Here," she announced.

Anders had a camp shovel in his pack that he had assembled and used now to moved dirt and stone out of the way as everyone else watched.

Egon listened to the voices in his head, but also the surroundings. Vorlothe was still around here somewhere, presumably licking his wounds. Egon had no doubt that the sword/demon would call to the Dwarf for rescue from them. Cletus might have been watching the excavations, but the Puck was almost vibrating with suppressed energy, probably just waiting for that idiot Harridan to step out and announce himself.

The Puck ran much deeper than Egon had given him any credit for, prior to this.

Quickly, Anders hit the original stone slab of the floor, more mosaics but perfectly flat and then polished over with a layer of clear enamel or something to seal it against time and the wear of armored boots.

He worked outward now, shifting and tossing things well away until he stopped with a thump.

"Ilvash?" he asked, stepping aside.

Egon drew his hammer now for something to keep his hands busy. Cletus noticed and nodded.

The other two were down on hands and knees now, scooping and brushing, until Ilvash sat back on her ankles.

"I think we've found it," she said.

Cletus prodded Egon on the knee, so they both approached the hole.

He could smell a patch of wild roses in the summer wind, emanating from the spot Anders had opened in poisoned dirt.

He knelt next to them and tapped with his hammer, as yet entirely unwilling to grasp an unknown magical blade again any time soon.

Clink. Tap. Clink.

Egon didn't have much oil left in his metaphorical lantern, but this was important, so he used a bit to open his senses, nearly blinding himself as he did. The light that filled the sky was purest white. So much better than the crimson haze that wanted to engulf him.

Egon slipped his hammer back into the loop on his belt and reached out a hand, grasping the blade they'd found near the tip and rocking it back and forth a little to loosen it in the soil. It broke free easily enough and he pulled it up into the air, point still centered on his chest rather than reaching for the pommel. But the blade was safe.

"Master Wilson, if you would?" he asked, tilting the blade towards the tallowmaster.

In the distance of his mind, Egon heard screaming, but that was just a demon awakening to his most-ancient foe. He smiled, both inwardly as well as out.

Anders Wilson gripped the handle. It had no name that the four of them had heard, but they had not researched this particular part of the legend. Cletus had heard of the map, stolen it, then recruited a team to go after it in the space of three days.

The sword glowed in the hands of the tallowmaster. Egon rose on sore knees and nodded.

Now he had two mysteries to solve: how to destroy the red blade, and what to do with the Captain's.

Oh, and that evil Dwarf bastard was still running around somewhere.

FIFTEEN
STARLIGHT

EGON LOOKED out the door of the tavern at the stars fading. In the east, the sun first suggested day arising soon. They had fled the palace back to the tavern via the underground tunnels, never seeing Vorlothe as they did, but nonetheless prepared to fight the little shit to the death if they did.

And with the white blade present, that might have been the outcome had he appeared.

"Should we sleep below?" Ilvash asked, standing behind the bar but still in the room with them.

"No," Egon said before any of the others could speak up. "It will be light soon enough. If I had greater faith, I'd say we walk back to Jojo, but there are still night hunters about. Let us rest up here for now and then move when the sun burns away some of the fog that lingers."

"Well said, my friend," Cletus replied. "Ilvash, we can spare a bit of our remaining power here to set warnings in place. I highly doubt that Egon could actually sleep short of some extremely powerful spells anyway, so we should be safe."

Egon nodded and settled himself on the ground, in front of the bar but with the others in the kitchen where they would be safe enough. Anders had laid out his bedroll on the trapdoor itself, so nobody would open it without waking the man.

Egon watched as the two casters went to work, slowly building magical threads around them. He had the red sword still with his pack, close but not too close. Anders Wilson held the Captain's blade against surprises.

A nap would not give him time to fully recover, but he could sleep later, once they had Jojo pointed in the direction of safety. For now, he meditated and prayed, eyes open and watching out the door for light to spill into the street.

Or dark things to approach.

"'Twill be fine, my friend," Cletus said, standing close when they had finished.

"How do we destroy that thing?" Egon asked. "It isn't merely a hunk of polished steel."

"I know, Egon the Bold," Cletus nodded. "You did a desperate thing, stopping Vorlothe from grasping it, and I had feared that it would be too much for even you, but I am pleased to know that my first instincts were correct in this matter. That someone others might call a mere Orc was made of sterner moral fiber than most of the people I have ever met."

"How old are you, Cletus?" Egon asked, aware that the other two had retired to the other room now.

Perhaps giving the two of them some privacy, however little it was?

"Older than many might take me for, Egon the Bold," the Puck grinned. "Like the Elves, my kind age slowly, so many take me for the young man I no longer am. But I am not so much older than you that I have forgotten what it means to set out on an adventure. As to destroying *Ediade*, you would still be a better one to determine that than I."

"They summoned a demon, Cletus," Egon explained. "But instead of giving him a Humanoid form, they cast him as a blade. He has the ability to warp minds, as you saw. I fought him but it was not enough."

"That was why you had friends, Egon," Cletus reminded him.

"I nearly killed Ilvash," he said. "Well, he did, but it would have been my hand."

"And you held him," the Puck reminded him. "Fought him to a standstill and that was something else for the legends that will come."

"If it was a made thing from a forge, we could just break it," Egon continued. "Angle it and strike with a hammer until it snapped. Or heat it and melt it down to an ingot. But there is no amount of heat that will soften that steel. I have wondered if we could just open a portal to hell and chuck him through, but nothing would stop another fool from bringing him back."

"Rest for now, then," Cletus offered. "There are other minds we might consult once we escape this dreary place.

Egon found himself alone in the front room. He sat perfectly still and listened to Anders snore quietly from the back room, so at least someone was able to sleep. He suspected that the other two were pretending, so as to not rouse the other.

He closed his eyes and prayed.

SIXTEEN

VISION

EGON FOUND himself in a strange place. Not the ruins of Gillanish nor even the *darkwilds*. The air was colder and there was snow on the ground in many places.

It felt like home.

He was on a path through a forest, a game trail pounded into the snow by passing elk and smaller creatures. There was light, but he could not see the sun to tell direction, so he picked the likelier of the two directions and started to walk.

Egon was used to walking. He had gone south without a horse, intent on learning the land by traversing it, rather than racing madly through on his course elsewhere. Only a few wagon rides from friendly farmers had helped him cover any of the distance to Teregossa from home.

The forest had that chill silence that came on at the first of morning after a hard blizzard, when all the creatures have nestled in for winter or flown south, and you might be the only person stupid enough to be up and about.

Not that such a description had ever applied to him, mind you.

Occasional snow fell from branches with whoofs of air,

and the crisp smell of pine needles filled him, but there was no smoke from a friendly campfire in the air, so he walked.

The path widened after a time. Not quite to a road, but sufficient that a wagon could clear the boles of trees on both sides. He did finally smell smoke, and let that guide him as he emerged into a clearing with a small cabin off to one side.

Small. Perhaps only one room, though he couldn't see the rear to judge the depth of it. A well off to one side with a bucket on a wheel. Grinding wheel in another spot, to sharpen knifes and shears. Firewood stacked against the side greater than his height and two layers deep to provide insulation against the wind and storm.

Egon mounted the stairs slowly and deliberately, rapping on the door without pushing and then stepping down onto the packed snow beyond the roof overhang.

He waited.

Eventually, the door opened, but he wasn't sure how much time might have passed. This was a dreamscape, so all things were possible. Or so it seemed.

The woman standing in the door was one he recognized. She had been mistaken for a merchant's wife in Teregossa, the one who had spoken up for him after that second ambush, when the city watch might have arrested him for brawling.

If she was not Brese Herself, the woman was an avatar of some sort.

Egon bowed his head to her and waited for the woman to speak.

"Your journey is incomplete," she said without preamble.

"I am aware, Mistress," Egon replied. "We have merely prevented the Dwarf from laying hands on the blade. Nothing more. I seek a way to destroy it. If it can be destroyed."

"It is power you could use," she said, but Egon shook his head abruptly.

"It is pure evil," he said. "I have felt the taste of the being within. Even were I to somehow constrain it, it would still be a soul-stealer. Some things are too dangerous to allow to remain."

"And you would know how to end *Ediade* as a being?" she asked.

Egon went to one knee. That felt even more appropriate, considering the circumstances.

"Prince Mahyrst failed, but was successful enough to buy us time," he said, looking up at the tall, Human woman. "The demon slept for a while, until Vorlothe woke him and I nearly fell in his path. He cannot be allowed, but I am not strong enough to destroy him by myself. For that, I will need help. I will need friends."

She smiled at him.

"Every soul that the sword has ever take remains in that blade, Egon the Bold," she said.

Egon felt the entire world go fuzzy around him, fading and shrinking as he somehow turned into a giant and raced across the sky.

He jolted awake as the sun crept into the tavern through the open remains of what had once been the front door. Cletus stood close by, as did Ilvash and Anders, the later holding a particular blade naked in his hands, as though wakened to flow instantly to battle.

"Are you well, lad?" the Human asked.

Egon smiled up at him, and then nodded to the sword.

"I think I know the way."

SEVENTEEN

UNICORN

EGON APPROACHED at the tail of their little column, as normal. Anders and his new sword led the way, with the two sorcerers between them for safety. Beyond Vorlothe, there might be all manner of things, but Egon and Anders had both agreed that the sun would drive some off, while the morning coolness would cause certain things to remain lethargic.

It would be the best time to elude pursuit.

Egon still watched backwards regularly, feeling eyes on him, but nothing emerged to threaten them.

Anders slowed as they got close, moving to cover behind a pile of rubble and beckoning the other to join him. Egon sat sideways and watched all directions.

"What is that?" Ilvash asked.

To Egon, it looked like a small pile of fur outside the stables where Jojo had been. Far too small to be their farting, hairy unicorn, but something that had not been there before. Egon noted several other similar piles, strewn about the street.

"Do you smell that?" he asked Anders.

The Human glanced at him with a bit of surprise and took a deeper smell of the air.

"Dead things," he replied.

"Evil things," Egon countered, wondering if the touch of *Ediade* that remained in his soul had forever tainted him. His sensitivity to such things seemed much heightened. "And dead."

"Let us exercise care and approach," Cletus said. "Jojo is one that can hopefully take care of herself."

They rose now and slid along the side of the boulevard, Egon with his hammer and Anders with Mahyrst's blade.

Egon kept watch as Anders inspected it.

"How the hell did such a thing make it this far north?" Anders grumbled.

"What have you found, Tallowmaster?" Cletus asked, stepping close.

"A pack of what look to my eye as hyenas, master wizard," Anders replied. "At least according to the descriptions I have encountered, having never met such things."

Egon moved to inspect one. Like Anders, he had never seen such a thing, but wouldn't have even been able to identify it.

Dog-like, sort of. Larger than a cat, at least, and heavy. Mangy pelt in golden brown. Heavy jaws.

"These are creatures of the tropical plains," Anders was explaining.

"We already know that the twisted magic of the region has caused things to mutate into forms none would have ever expected," Ilvash offered scientifically. "Could the magic have worked on some rodent or small creature?"

A whoomph of sound caused all heads to snap up and look to the left, weapons ready.

Jojo stomped out of the stables with great disdain,

walking right up to Anders and sniffing him hard once, before her enormous tongue came out like a cat's to swipe at his face. She inspected the rest of then with her nose, pausing to consider him twice.

"He's fine, furball," Anders said to her, reaching up under her chin to scratch.

"So would be best assume that the pack sought to attack her and got stomped into the dirt for their troubles?" Cletus asked brightly.

"This one was gored," Anders pointed. "Those two were squished. Most likely, since she has no visible injuries."

Jojo snorted. Or sneezed. Something. Then she leaned against Anders a little.

"And I think this little lady would like to go home now," the tallowmaster laughed.

"As would we all," Cletus laughed.

They laughed and started to organize. The wagon was still in place, though it appeared that Jojo had shoved it at least once at some point, moving it twenty feet closer to home. Still, she backed right into place and let Anders hitch her while Egon helped everyone put packs and things into the back.

At one point, something made him stop and turn back to look at the palace. The distance was impossibly great, but he saw movement on a tower and knew that Vorlothe was watching. Had just summoned something with his power that would let him track them into the wastes.

That he would remain a thorn in their sides.

"My boy?" Cletus asked, suddenly right next to him.

Egon pointed, though he doubted that the Puck could see that far.

What connected Egon to Vorlothe was more than mere distance could diminish.

"Will he follow us?" Ilvash asked.

"One can hope, dear lady," Cletus said.

"We want him to?" she asked.

"With your immense assistance, I was able to thwart the Dwarf in his quest to recover the blade," Cletus responded. "Who know what other things might have fallen in that battle, or perhaps from the hands of a dead adventurer subsequently? If the Harridan seeks us out, he is not remaining here to perhaps find a worthwhile second place trophy."

"But he is still a threat?" she asked/said.

"Indubitably," Cletus nodded. "Less so, with the blade in our possession, as well as the second blade, but some greater power has made pacts with the Dwarf. We approach a terrible endgame now, wherein our foe is likely to grow more desperate with every step we take to elude him now. Egon, you must be on your guard at all times. We three will do what we can, but there will be limits."

Egon nodded and turned his back on the Dwarf for now. Somehow he knew that there was no speed that Jojo could carry them that would be sufficient to outrun Vorlothe, but they needed to be away from the city and all the other fell things that might be called by a petulant and fuming punk.

Anything that took up the sword would be sufficient for the demon to dominate. And conquer.

EIGHTEEN

DARKWILDS

EGON STOOD watch on a small rise, reaching out with magical senses as well as Orcish vision that could see into the dark farther than the others. The terrain was still flat behind them and slowly rising as Anders guided them up into a range of low hills and long valleys. Around them, the trees had begun to press in some, thought the road was still broad and flat from the magic and engineering of the ancients. The road they had come in upon originally was not an option, unless they wanted to spend time bridging the gap they had created, then facing off with the monster therein.

A light snow had fallen recently enough that they were all bundled up now in spare sweaters and scarves. Egon had stripped his armor off entirely just long enough to add a layer of wool his mother had knitted, so he was cozy and even moved with less jingling now.

The day had been long, but Egon had managed a good nap in the back of the wagon. Not enough, but he was at least sharp for now. Nearby, Jojo was ripping low branches off a fir tree and happily munching, while Anders gathered fallen limbs for the fire that Cletus was tending. Ilvash had been raised in a magical tower, but she had at least learned how to cook, so Cletus let her handle that.

Egon simply watched.

A smell intruded on his brain. Sharp and crisp, the scent of fir trees after winter had hit.

He started with recognition and muttered a profanity under his breath.

Not far enough under his breath, as Ilvash tuned to look him square in the face. Egon felt the blush burn his ears.

"Cletus," she said simply, nodding in Egon's direction when the Puck looked up from his fire.

"What is it, Egon?" Cletus asked standing now and walking closer.

"That vision I had last night, when we were in the tavern," he explained. He'd told them most of it. The important parts, at least. He gestured to the trees around them. "This was the smell. Different from the valleys up north because the trees are another breed."

"Indeed, much more evergreens in your homeland," Cletus agreed. "Is this the path you found yourself on when the Goddess called you?"

Egon took a few steps to his left, ignoring the trail behind them now to circle the wagon and the furry unicorn. Ahead, the snow was unbroken. It would be easy for a Dwarf to track them here, but that was part of Cletus's plan.

Draw him away from Gillanish, where he might find all manner of allies.

There would be other things in the trees, but many of those would merely be wild and dangerous, rather than active servants of evil.

Egon took a few more steps. Jojo wasn't tall, but her solid mass would let her breast her way through even a heavier snow. Given all the time in the world, they would be better served to have a sleigh instead of wheels now.

The white cold he stomped through was only as deep as his boots, though, not threatening to slip inside for now, but he still had oilskin gaiters protecting things.

He drew a deep breath in through his nose and nodded. It smelled the same. Not home, as much as the cold and trees wanted to remind him.

Egon nodded to Cletus where the Puck had remained in tracks that taller people had tromped down.

"Well at least she knew which path we would take," Anders chuckled. "Let us hope that she will guide us. Where will this road lead?"

"In the vision, I came out on a forest game trail barely wide enough to walk," Egon said. "As I walked, it slowly grew wider, but still not as wide as this."

"The map shows that the road wanders up this valley, over a pass, and then into a second," Anders nodded. "From there, we can either head south again and eventually get back onto the Teregossa road, or possibly look deeper into the mountains for the ancient passes that supposedly still lead to Egon's homeland, but I would rather not try them this late in the season unless we had to."

"Agreed," Cletus said. "Let us pay attention for any side roads that might have been preserved by the Goddess for weary travelers, shall we not?"

Egon nodded and returned to his spot behind the wagon. The breeze was so slight as to nonexistent, but he could feel Vorlothe back there, perhaps with whatever had remained of his wolves like some Wild Hunt like the easterners supposedly worshiped and feared.

The fire would not deter them, but it was far enough off the road itself as to be not immediately visible until someone got close. And Jojo was still grumpy at anything that moved, so Egon didn't think that anyone could sneak up easily.

Not counting a Harridan and whatever powers his patron might grant him.

A howling in the distance made everyone start, but Anders just looked up and shrugged.

"Many miles off, carried up the valley by the cold air," he said.

Probably, that would be reassuring, except that everyone understood that such creatures might be hunting them.

Still, Cletus and Ilvash scraped off the snow and enchanted a circle large enough to include Jojo as well as the fire, then they all retired to a spot under the trees where the ground was still covered with brown pine needles, with little snow blown in.

He would keep watch for now, and Anders would sleep, then they would trade later.

"They're still coming," Egon said quietly as the others settled.

"Of that, I have no doubt," Cletus said. "But we made good time today, so I expect that they will catch up tomorrow."

Egon saw the grim determination in the Puck's eyes and understood just how ugly tomorrow was likely to get.

NINETEEN
SNOW

IT HAD SNOWED AGAIN while Egon has slept. For a few moments, as he drank some tea and waited for stew to warm, he was back in that dream vision, ready to trudge. The new depth was much closer to what it had been in his dream, almost to his knees now and likely impassable to either Cletus or Ilvash, at least without him breaking a trail for them.

Jojo snorted and wallowed in it, almost like a child blowing bubbles, but this was closer to her ideal winter, so he wouldn't begrudge the rhinoceros that.

Still, Egon couldn't help but glance back up their road regularly. Nothing was yet visible with the sun just barely over the eastern horizon.

"We will move early today," Cletus announced. "I have done a few divinations that suggest a place we can defend, ahead of us on this road, while others confirm that Vorlothe has found friends with which to pursue us. He and a band of wolves are on foot, but limited by his stature, else they would be nearly upon us by now. Time it short, but not critical."

Egon nodded and ate quickly, as did the others. Even

Jojo picked up on the tension and did not fuss about getting hitched.

The sword called him when Egon climbed up into the wagon.

So easy to just pull it out and unwrap it. Grasp that pommel in his hand and he'd be able to slaughter all of Vorlothe's wolves and then take the Dwarf's soul forever to power his new conquests.

It took a long moment and gritted teeth to ignore that siren call and turn his back, feet dangling off the tailgate and crossbow in his lap. Ilvash sat next to him.

"Everything all right?" she asked quietly as they rolled through and over snow banks.

"The blade wants to be free," Egon replied. "Wants me to take it up so it can conquer the world again."

"Could you control it?" she asked, slipping into more of an academic role.

"Unlikely," Egon laughed harshly. "The last time it took me completely."

"You were also surprised," the young woman noted. "And fought against him. You even managed to break free."

"Luck, as much as anything," Egon shrugged. "If we weren't being pursued, there are other things I might try, but we are likely to be desperate soon."

"He is only one Dwarf," Ilvash bristled a little. "And a harridan at that."

"He knows about the four of us, though," Egon countered. "And still chases, so he believes that he will be somehow sufficient for the task. If I were you, I would not rely on illusion, as he seems to be able to see through it somehow."

"Oh, I have things I have not done yet," Ilvash grinned.

He grinned back, hoping that it would be enough.

Otherwise, he might have to take hold of the blade, if only to prevent the Dwarf from using it.

THE ROAD WAS AT ONCE obvious, and hidden, but to Egon it stood out like a lit candle in a window to guide someone in the darkness. Anders felt the same way, because he stopped well short.

"Here, Egon?" he asked with a glance back.

Everyone unloaded and looked. It was a gap in the trees, barely wide enough for the wagon and running back only a short distance before it turned. The snow on the way was hard and unmarred, even by rabbit tracks.

But his vision agreed.

"Here," he nodded, stopping to remember. "Not that deep into the trees, either. It will run back for perhaps one hundred yards, twisting a bit, and then open onto a meadow of sorts."

"Excellent," Cletus announced. "Let us see to it, then."

Everyone loaded up and rode as Jojo got them into the trees. Egon thought he could hear a howl in the distance, but it might have been the wind.

Down a ways, the trees pinched in, as if resenting their intrusion to the last, and then withdrew in a familiar meadow.

Egon hopped off even before the wagon stopped rolling and walked over to where the well had stood in his dream. It was nearly collapsed now, the wood top mostly rotted and the masonry holding the stones together cracked. For some reason, the bucket remained intact, but it had been set to one side and was half buried by the snow.

He grabbed a rock from nearby and dropped it in,

listening as it splashed below rather than cracking ice, so the water was deep enough to still be present.

He nodded to himself and turned to the cabin.

In his vision, there had been paint on edges and frames, showing off the stain where the wood had been sealed by an expert artisan, but again, that had happened a long time ago. Six centuries, perhaps? Maybe, if there was enough magic involved. Maybe less, and folks had hidden here in the trees and survived for a few generations after everything in the lowlands had fallen?

That felt right. Eventually, the monsters in the forests had grown too dangerous or too bold, and anyone who could had fled to the perimeters of the old empire, crossing rivers, mountains, or a swampy waste in the southeast.

Only the evil had remained.

The snow was shallower here. Maybe as deep as the tops of his boots again, where it had been nearly to his thighs in places on the roadway in. Egon assumed magic sheltering this place, just as it had that tavern. Enough had remained behind, at least.

The cabin door was closed when he stepped onto the porch, Cletus and Ilvash close behind him and Anders watching the wagon, Jojo, and the trail they had entered on.

Egon took a deep breath and pushed it open with his hammer, unsure what he would see. His shield was just intact enough to perhaps last one more battle, assuming nobody hit it particularly hard. He had it on his arm anyway, a comfortable weight.

The interior was intact, such as it was. A fireplace on the left wall, bracketed by shuttered windows letting in twin beams of thin light. A table with two benches where six might crowd companionably and a stuffed sofa more likely to be seen in a big city was facing the fire.

Egon stepped in and checked the corners. He'd been

right about the depth, showing off a sleeping nook with a made bed and a trunk, plus another shuttered window. On the right, a place for travelers to rest or livestock to overnight indoors.

There was precious little dust in here, even on the shelves that were empty of the jars and bins that they might have once held. Whoever had lived here had taken the time to pack almost everything and leave, abandoning things too big for a wagon or sleigh in their motion. Or perhaps just taking what they could carry on their backs or horse.

He walked to the windows and noted that the shutters were designed to hold winter at bay, rather than angry Dwarves or demonic wolves. They would not hold any longer than necessary for someone to chop them open with an ax or slip a knife in and lift a bar.

He grunted and noted that Cletus was nearby. Egon gestured to the thing, but Cletus grinned and gestured with his hand. A light flashed.

"Perhaps now you might try again?" the Puck laughed.

Egon noted that the bar holding the two shutters appeared to be made of iron now, rather than wood, and extended past the edges in the inside to where it seemed attached to the frame directly. Egon nodded to the others and continued inspecting as Cletus moved on to get the others.

The floor underfoot was packed dirt, rather than wood. Cold in the winter, but no space for rodents to easily move around except by tunneling, and Egon suspected that the owners had kept cats. He moved to the door.

"Anders, if she might fit through the doorway, we could bed Jojo down inside, away from trouble," he called, watching the impact of the words on the tallowmaster. "Not much we can do about the supplies in the wagon, except go hunting on our way home and find you more things."

Anders laughed.

"Having her to pull us is better than us having to pull the wagon, my friend," he said, moving to the rhinoceros and talking quietly to her.

The others started moving gear inside, confident now that the walls might hold long enough for the two wizards to keep burglars at bay while Egon held the door itself. Or perhaps the porch, as he would need space to swing his hammer and it would be better to do that where he could put his height and armor to use.

The grinding wheel was the last thing to inspect before he began to flatten what snow was left in front of the house. He didn't even need to use any of the power Brese had gifted him to know that it had been a magical thing in its time. The entire mechanism looked as good as new, in spite of decades or centuries in the weather. Egon put his weight against it a little, just to see if he could move it, but the thing weighed at least as much as he did, so sturdy it was built.

Still, if they could get that into the wagon somehow, he would happily walk home so as to not overload the axles.

He turned and watched as Jojo wriggled her broad hips through the doorway with a snort of indignation Egon would have more expected from one of his mother's cats, but she got inside.

Good. As long as he managed to kill all the wolves and the Dwarf, the others would be able to get home easily enough, even without him.

Without him? Egon weighed his odds and decided that he had to prepare for death here. A forge cleric was focused on the creation of things. Using fire, steel, and patience to create art.

But at the same time, destruction was just as necessary, as you had to take old things that were broken and melt them down and hammer them into new shapes.

His shield, for instance, would probably be better so demolished.

"Egon," Ilvash called, causing him to turn sharply.

Her voice held a note of...wonder?

Egon saw her emerging from the door, holding a round shield. Wooden, with an steel rim and boss, in the pattern of the tribes that usually lived further to the east.

Like the rest of the cabin, it appeared almost new, the wood gleaming with polish and the metal shining as it caught the morning light occasionally breaking through the clouds.

"This was on the bed," she said, holding it out to him. "Under the blanket."

Egon cursed himself for a fool. He'd forgotten to clear the entire space, impatient to get Jojo safe.

"Anything else there?" he asked.

"No," she shook her head. "Was it left just for us? It seems new."

"This is probably ancient," he replied, taking his battered shield off to lean against his leg and hanging his hammer from his belt so he could study this new artifact.

Brese's symbol was etched into the rim, over and over again. Probably with acid, but the craft to do that was something even a master artisan might hesitate before pursuing. He opened his mind to it and noted that it had been enchanted by a master at some point, after at least one other master had crafted such a thing.

He slung in onto his forearm and felt how perfectly it hung, even though he was a foot taller than the average Human who had one resided in these lands.

Left for him indeed. She had made sure he would come here and find it.

A sound caught Egon's ear. A yip like a dog.

"They come," he called to everyone, grabbing his old

shield and placing it into Ilvash's hands as he chivied her towards the cabin and whatever safety the building might grant them.

If nothing else, a wolf getting inside would be facing Jojo, who would treat them even worse than she had the hyenas.

For now, trouble had found them.

TWENTY

WOLVES

EGON TOOK his spot in front of the porch, where the overhang didn't bother him on an overhead swing. It would allow a wolf a chance to get up there unseen and pounce on him, so he would need to pay attention.

Anders stood in the doorway itself with the other sword, with a bard and an enchanter behind him, all prepared for violence.

Egon had rested some. Not enough to be back to where he might have been, but sufficient unto the day. This would be a time of steel, rather than magic, at least for him.

Let the others rely on tools outside themselves. What he needed was already deep in his soul, a forge quietly resting after a long night, as a silly third son prince woke early, completed his prayers, and set to working the bellows as the masters sought to teach him.

The yips were louder now. And more of them. A pack of the dark beasts coming, excited for a midday meal that the Dwarf had no doubt promised them.

Fresh Orc, but only if they could take it.

Egon set his feet and dug them into the frozen ground a

little. They would be coming at him from all sides, so he would need to simply stand as a breakwater protecting the harbor at first, trusting his armor and Brese's new shield to protect him until the tide turned and ebbed sideways around him.

He'd never seen the ocean, but bards like Cletus had traveled to his father's Court. Well, not like Cletus. Egon suspected that there were precious few of that caliber, but the roads often ran heavy with wandering storytellers in the summers.

He spied movement through the trees. Dark shadows racing madly along but silent now. The smell of the winter sap hung heavy about him as time itself seemed to come to a stop.

"Egon, prepare yourself for a little something as a surprise for our friends," Cletus called.

He nodded, but didn't dare look.

Instead, he felt something start at his feet and work up his body. Looking down, there was a glow as winter taffy seemed to swallow him, but it did not impeded his feet or hands in any way.

A magical shield of some sort. So be it. Anything to let him hold this line just a little longer and kill that many more wolves before they dragged him down.

He growled as the first one came into sight and skidded to a halt.

Even a wolf might know a moment of unquiet, facing an armored foe who had no fear whatsoever. He would need his whole pack around him to gather courage, just like the yapping hounds of the average tavern must work themselves up to a fury.

More appeared, loping to a halt until there were more than a dozen ranged in a crescent moon with the horns pointed towards him.

Then the Dwarf appeared.

He was still the frothing, little shit that Egon had met coming back from the outhouse, on that morning that had first started this adventure. Maybe his beard had gotten even wilder now, but that might be due to not bathing in a year.

His gear was more torn, perhaps from madly chasing through the woods and dancing for his master's pleasure.

Brese demanded quiet prayers and solid commitment to excellence. Nothing more.

Warriors of the mind as much as the body, standing against evil.

It was a pity they hadn't had more time to prepare for this, but Egon would make the most of what he had.

He took a step towards the wolves, hammer up and shield forward.

The closest one shied a little, but only for a moment.

"Kill him!" Vorlothe snarled, pointing with that stupid ax of his.

The wolves howled something back and charged.

Egon set his feet and braced, shield forward and hammer back. Rather than let them tackle him down with their mass, he shifted to his right as they closed, swinging hammer and shield to disrupt movement, rather than trying to damage them.

It worked, for a moment, as their very numbers told against them, bodies colliding and snapping at each other in their wild haste to taste Orc.

And then something exploded.

Egon shook his head to clear it and found himself sitting on his ass in the cold snow, unsure how he'd gotten there. His ears rang with something like a mild concussion mixed with a bad hangover. Vorlothe's power must have gone up an entire scale.

Except that the Dwarf was just as stunned when Egon

locked eyes with him, still over by the entrance to the meadow.

Around him, the wolves had suffered the brunt of it, scorched and still smoldering in places, blasted sideways into the snow and whining in pain.

Egon staggered to his feet and glanced at the doorway. Ilvash was down on one knee, with Cletus holding her upright. Had she just channeled that much power?

He hadn't even realized the woman HAD that much arcane might at her disposal, but apparently the costs were high, as she might have used it all in one blast.

Still, the wolves got it worse than he did.

Egon stumbled to the nearest and crushed its skull before the beast could right itself. A second went a moment later.

"NO!" Vorlothe screamed and charged, so Egon ignored the others.

He would ask later what the woman had done, and thank her.

For now, that glowing ax was going to be a problem.

Like before, Egon feinted with the shield, as though he was going to let that Dwarf simply step into a two-handed, overhead blow with something glowing that brightly and let his shield take the brunt.

At the last moment, he slipped to the side and hammered another wolf instead.

Vorlothe was overextended, as normal. Nobody had ever taught the fool how to properly fight with an ax. He buried it into the snow and frozen dirt when Egon wasn't there.

The explosion was almost as powerful as whatever Ilvash had done before, knocking them both sideways and skidding them across the snow.

Egon lost his hammer in the mess, the snow swallowing it into one of the banks piled up as bodies were tossed every which way. He scrambled to his feet, still holding the shield but now armed with nothing greater about him than a belt knife, as the remaining few wolves circled and began taking half-lunges to nip at him.

They were oversized cats now, a whole pack playing with a single mouse.

"Egon," Anders called.

He could see where the man was intent on charging into battle, but he wore no armor better than leather with a few rivets. The wolves would be on him in an instant, and then Cletus a moment later.

"No!" Egon yelled, batting at a snout that got too close to him and thwapping it hard on the nose with his shield. "You stay there and protect the others."

Cletus did something, but the bolt merely bounced off that barrier that Vorlothe seemed to have around him against magic.

Had the Dwarf and the Puck been at this for so long that they knew each other that well?

Vorlothe stood facing the cabin now, waving his ax at the other three. Egon was facing wolves across his entire front as they backed him. His butt touched the grinding wheel that had brought him such lust earlier and he held. That would at least cover him from behind for a bit.

Another snap, but the creature withdrew before Egon could hit it, and then another almost got his knife hand before he realized it.

They would kill him in a matter of moments.

Cletus tried something else, but his magic seemed more geared towards supporting his friends and sneaking in places, rather than standing on a battlefield with another arcanist and blasting each other. That was why Ilvash had been recruited, but she had used up everything blasting the wolves the first time.

Anders was no warrior. Jojo would make a puddle of some, but only after the others had fallen.

Vorlothe turned sideways enough to taunt him now.

"Long have I waited for a moment such as this," the Dwarf called theatrically.

Egon hated monologues. He slipped his knife back into its scabbard.

He sighed and opened his mind.

Time to die, one way or the other.

Egon the Bold held out his hand and called to a demon.

In the cabin, *Ediade* awoke from his sulking slumber and turned his gaze this direction with a terrible laugh.

Evil has no friends. Only today's allies who will be tomorrow's victims.

The blade wriggled free of the cloth around it and flew true to Egon's hand.

Time seemed to stop around them. Silence reigned supreme, as even the birds in the trees held their breaths in awe and fear.

Brese had warned him that it would come to this. He had to trust her.

Ediade ripped at his mind, but Egon held firm.

We must kill the Dwarf and his allies first, let they steal your prizes, Egon thought at the thing gibbering in his mind.

It was like pouring cold molasses into his tea on a winter morning, but the demon subsided.

For now. For the promise of blood and souls.

Egon knew that he would fall before the creature's will eventually. No mortal had the strength to resist for long.

He didn't need long.

Ediade swooped right and left and a pair of wolves fell, sundered in twain and smoking.

Vorlothe's eyes had grown huge with surprise, tinged perhaps with fear.

The demon slew another pair of wolves in another eyeblink, and began laughing wildly as the last two shrank back from him.

Nothing could stop *Ediade* now. He would take the Dwarf's soul, and with it all the power the dark one had gifted him.

A bolt from the cabin struck the nearer wolf in the haunches, burning it and tipping it over. The last one turned to bolt and *Ediade* drank his soul down.

Only he and a fool of a Dwarf held the battlefield now. He would kill the one and then take the others, the ones who thought they might be champions of law and goodness.

Ediade sneered at the mass of them and stepped at the Dwarf.

The fool stumbled backwards now, ax before him. His eyes started to glow and *Ediade* slashed upward with his sword, intercepting some eldritch blast meant to twist his mind.

Fool, you cannot have this mind. It is mine for the owning, as is this body. I will take this Orc and bring down everything in fire to make them pay for six centuries they left me locked in a stone coffin.

Ediade advanced another step, slashing at the Dwarf. Toying with him like the wolves had toyed with the Orc before.

Vorlothe swung his ax. *Ediade* blocked it with his shield, then felt fire engulf his entire left arm as magical sparks flew in every direction.

His arm continued burning, and *Ediade* realized that the bitch goddess had laid a trap. The shield was a holy weapon in its own right. It would burn him even as the sword that the Human male carried.

Ediade recognized the blade. Mahyrst had carried it that

day. Died with it in his hands, even as he had sacrificed his life to kill the Elf Arinwa Hollenc.

Ediade silently promised the Human a slow and painful death.

Slaughter the Dwarf and then the Puck. Torture the male. Rape the Human woman before cutting her throat.

This world was going to be so much fun.

But the shield burned.

Ediade slipped it from his arm and dropped it into the snow as the Dwarf recovered. Like the Dwarf, he gripped his pommel with two hands and swung, blade meeting shaft at the top of their arcs.

A sword would have severed the haft of an normal ax, but Vorlothe's was enchanted. Not as great as *Ediade*, but sufficient. They exploded outward with a flash of light and power that staggered both figures backwards a step before they could recover.

Ediade heard the Orc whisper in his head now. He tried to ignore the fool, but his words made sense, married with memories.

The idiot Dwarf liked the overhand blow married with a terrible smiting of power loaded. The Orc had seen it several times now.

Ediade stepped forward and feinted at the Dwarf with a jab. Vorlothe sidestepped and smacked the sword, turning that into a round about arc behind his head for a tree-felling chop.

Ediade watched the blow swing, timed it, and the stepped back, letting the glowing, razor-sharp edge pass him by no more than an inch.

He jammed the tip of the sword into the Dwarf's stomach as the fool's ax was trapped in the frozen ground, and felt the Dwarf scream.

They always screamed. That was the best part, sharing

that moment of knowledge with them that they are about to die and then both of them watching as *Ediade* swallowed their soul.

Vorlothe fought it. They always did. Even the dark one had not prepared his harridan for something so drastic.

The screams were like music in a poor demon's ears.

Eventually, they stopped. Vorlothe's shriveled corpse smoked slightly at his feet, barely bleeding at all.

Ediade savored the moment. He hadn't consumed a being of power in so very long.

He looked up now at the Human. The male with Mahyrst's sword, standing defensively in the doorway, like that would help him at all.

Ediade laughed and took a step forward.

Or tried to.

No, the Orc voice said simply. You will not have them.

Fool, you cannot stop me, Ediade snarled back. *You are not my equal. None of you are ever my equal.*

True, the Orc nodded in their mind. *But I learned a powerful thing, sharing your mind with you, Ediade the Demon-borne. I know how to defeat you.*

YOU ARE TOO WEAK!!!

Again, the Orc nodded. It was almost serene, but *Ediade* could not move their body.

Was that the Orc's expectation? That the others would be able to slay the body while the Orc tried to hold it still? He would fail. All living creatures wanted to survive. Fought death to the end.

He would flinch, and in doing so, his grip would weaken. Then *Ediade* would be free of that grasping hand.

No, the Orc shook his head. *I thought about that, too. I would fail. Any of us would fail. But you have forgotten one important thing, demon.*

WHAT?!?

Every man who has ever died by your hand is still in here somewhere, the Orc explained in a calm, quiet voice. *Prince Mahyrst, I require your aid.*

Suddenly, a second being appeared in the snow beside them. Human. Tall. Almost as big as the Orc.

Angry.

Ediade recognized the man. Had slain him once upon a time. This one was only interesting because he had been strong enough to kill *Ediade*'s vessel before falling into the blade and waiting in limbo for six centuries.

The Human smiled.

Egon the Bold, I am come, he said in a strong voice.

Ediade felt hands on his mind. Human hands grappling with his mind and forcing him to turn his attention from the Orc.

Their body began to walk. One slow, painful step at a time, it turned away from the last three victims as *Ediade* howled.

You cannot defeat me, the demon screamed. *Not even two of you. I will win out eventually.*

The body took another staggering stride away from the cabin as *Ediade* fought Egon the Bold and Prince Mahyrst of Karnegriand, warrior captain of the western armies.

Egon you must do it now, Mahyrst gasped, struggling with a demon as slippery as an eel.

Egon found himself momentarily free and in control of the flesh he had been born to. He took the last stride and swung the sword with all his might, slamming the flat of the blade into the grinding wheel in a flash of light.

TWENTY-ONE
THE BOLD

EGON AWOKE WITH A JOLT. For the first time in days, there were no whispers in the back of his mind, coveting flesh and promising power if he would only take up the crimson sword.

Anders knelt next to him and a fire burned nearby.

He was in the cabin. Jojo snorted a greeting from across the room as he sat up.

"How long?" Egon asked, seeing Cletus and Ilvash across the way.

Where a demon-possessed Orc couldn't get to them quickly, he realized. Anders had Mahyrst's sword in hand.

"A few hours, my impossibly bold fellow," Cletus said now, striding across the room and drawing Ilvash in his wake. "I had not expected it, but you found a way to end a great and terrible evil forever."

Egon nodded and rolled to one side. Anders pulled him to his feet, and then held him upright when he would have toppled again immediately.

"Remind me not to do that again," Egon told his three friends.

"I will," Cletus grinned. "But you and I both know how foolhardy such a promise might be, Egon the Bold. You would not let it stop you."

Egon nodded. The Puck was right. Brese had picked him from among all her champions and set his feet to wandering. Had placed a Puck and a harridan athwart his path.

Or he theirs, perhaps?

"How is the grinding wheel?" Egon asked.

Anders laughed and led him out the door an onto the porch. The afternoon sun was quickly waning, but the light was sufficient to see a crater in the ground where the wheel had once been. Bodies of wolf and Dwarf were stacked like cordwood on the far side of the clearing, back under the trees a little where their presence wouldn't poison the good magic that remained.

Egon shuddered.

"What do you need, lad?" Anders asked.

"A little food, a little wine, and maybe an entire day to sleep," Egon replied. "I feel like you dragged me here from Teregossa behind the wagon right this moment."

"I'm with him," Ilvash said in a tired voice. "Let's sleep for a day before we attempt the road home."

"Not sure about the weather," Anders said, looking at the sky. "Feels like a storm is coming."

Egon started to say something, but Cletus cut him off.

"The snow will hold off long enough," the Puck said, staring into Egon's eyes.

Egon wasn't sure how the Puck could be so certain, but he shared that certainty.

The winter would hold off long enough for them to get to Harhn. After that, nobody would know, but Egon did know that he'd be back in the spring.

There were more things that needed to be defeated, living

in those ruins, if the rest of the world was going to grow up to replace all that had been lost.

They just needed a few heroes out front, showing them the way.

ABOUT THE AUTHOR

Blaze Ward writes science fiction in the Alexandria Station universe (Jessica Keller, The Science Officer, The Story Road, etc.) as well as several other science fiction universes, such as Star Dragon, the Dominion, and more. He also writes odd bits of high fantasy with swords and orcs. In addition, he is the Editor and Publisher of *Boundary Shock Quarterly Magazine.* You can find out more at his website www.blazeward.com, as well as Facebook, Goodreads, and other places.

Blaze's works are available as ebooks, paper, and audio, and can be found at a variety of online vendors. His newsletter comes out regularly, and you can also follow his blog on his website. He really enjoys interacting with fans, and looks forward to any and all questions—even ones about his books!

Never miss a release!
If you'd like to be notified of new releases, sign up for my newsletter.

http://www.blazeward.com/newsletter/

Buy More!
Did you know that you can buy directly from my website?

https://www.blazeward.com/shop/

Connect with Blaze!

Web: www.blazeward.com
Boundary Shock Quarterly (BSQ):
https://www.boundaryshockquarterly.com/

ABOUT KNOTTED ROAD PRESS

Knotted Road Press fiction specializes in dynamic writing set in mysterious, exotic locations.

Knotted Road Press non–fiction publishes autobiographies, business books, cookbooks, and how–to books with unique voices.

Knotted Road Press creates DRM–free ebooks as well as high–quality print books for readers around the world.

With authors in a variety of genres including literary, poetry, mystery, fantasy, and science fiction, Knotted Road Press has something for everyone.

Knotted Road Press
www.KnottedRoadPress.com